Poppy and Mary Ellen
All Fed Up
Book Two of the Frankenmuth Murder Mysteries

Readers are encouraged to go to www.MissionPointPress.com to contact the author
or to find information on how to buy this book in bulk at a discounted rate.

MISSION POINT PRESS

Published by Mission Point Press
2554 Chandler Rd.
Traverse City, MI 49696
(231) 421–9513
www.MissionPointPress.com

ISBN: 978-1-965278-09-3
Library of Congress Control Number: 2024921282
Printed in the United States of America

POPPY AND MARY & ELLEN ALL FED UP

BOOK TWO OF THE FRANKENMUTH MURDER MYSTERIES

MAH JONGG
TOURNEY

FISCHER

FRANKENMUTH
Museum & Gift Shop

BY ROZ WEEDMAN AND SUSAN TODD

PROMISE TO OUR READERS FROM THE AUTHORS:
NO DOGS DIE

For Mary Anne Ackerman
1957 – 2024

She inspired us all by her example that
"All of us should listen with respect and
genuine interest to everyone's story."

This story is for you, Mary Anne.

CONTENTS

1: Bootsie Comes to Town

Mary Ellen Freeman parked her little silver-blue convertible behind Fischer Hall in Frankenmuth, one of the top tourist towns in Michigan. It was famous for chicken, festivals, and a lively downtown filled with German architecture. She smoothed her short white hair. Mary Ellen loved living there and was delighted to see all the spring decorations brightening the shops. Even though early March in Michigan was not always spring-like, she had an optimistic nature and wore a pink sweater, pink-flowered blouse, slacks, and her signature Crocs—pink, of course.

As she got out of her car, she spotted Munchie List over by the Riverwalk. Munchie was a large, shaggy dog who often got loose and needed help getting home. Mary Ellen pulled out her phone and texted Poppy Lutz, her literal partner in crime. Along with being a co-owner of their private-investigation service, Poppy had a side hustle of locating missing dogs and getting them home. Munchie was a regular.

"Poppy, Munchie is behind Fischer Hall if you want to come and get him. He doesn't seem to be holding a detached hand, so I think it's a regular pickup." Mary Ellen was alluding to last year's murders in Frankenmuth that the two investigators helped solve, along with their friend Barney Mead. Munchie had discovered a key piece of evidence—a disembodied hand. That was going to remain a Frankenmuth story forever.

Mary Ellen walked through the front door of Fischer Hall and was grateful that a couple of tables and chairs had been set up to see how the room would work for the Mah Jongg tournament she was planning. Mah Jongg, a game invented in China and adapted to an American form, was played with tiles and an annual card created by the National Mah Jongg League in New York City that displayed over fifty choices of winning hands. Instead of playing cards, Mah Jongg players matched tiles in their hands with one of the annual card choices. It was a difficult enough game that it took a while to catch on. Mary Ellen had loved the game from the beginning. She had studied it, played online, and become a proficient player. She was, informally, the Maven of the Muth.

On her Mah Jongg blog, she had been in contact with a lady from Grand Rapids, on the west side of Michigan, and suggested a small, one-day tournament. Bootsie Van der Veer had posed this to her group, and they all agreed a tournament would be a great deal of fun. Today, Bootsie, who was in Frankenmuth on business ahead of the tournament, had agreed to meet Mary Ellen at Fischer Hall to iron out all the details. As the host of the first meeting, Mary Ellen made a schedule and dinner plans, organized a luncheon for the next day, and collected prizes. She also created a packet with all the times and events, including a calendar to keep everyone organized.

When the door opened, Mary Ellen turned around and said, "Welcome. I assume you are Bootsie Van der Veer?" She was addressing a medium-tall lady with light brown hair, a camel coat, a tan scarf, and indeed, boots.

Bootsie nodded. Mary Ellen walked quickly toward her.

"It's so nice to meet you. Did you have any trouble finding the place? I think this hall will be perfect for our tournament."

"It's fine," said Bootsie.

Mary Ellen waited a beat and dove right in with her packet. "I understand most of you will be staying at the Marv Herzog Hotel right up the road. It has a really lovely view of the river off the lobby. It's convenient to the hall, and I have made dinner reservations at Zehnder's for Friday evening, after the Meet and Greet at the Marv Herzog. Everything is within walking distance. Would you like to sit down and review the schedule of events?"

"No, I'll take the packet and look it over," said Bootsie.

"I think you said you were here on business, which is what, if I might ask?" Mary Ellen was trying hard to figure this lady out.

"Lighting. May I have the packet?"

"Oh, how interesting—like lamps and chandeliers?"

"Lighting, yes." Bootsie had her hand out.

"Well, here's the packet. Message me if you have any questions. I'll see you and your group next Friday."

"Thank you, Mary Ellen." And with that Bootsie walked out the door.

Mary Ellen was left standing in the middle of Fischer Hall with an amazed look on her face. The door opened again, and Mary Ellen thought Bootsie had come back to finish the conversation, but it was Poppy, readjusting her wig (she liked variety in her hair and had an array of them to choose from). Munchie had knocked her current wig askew while she encouraged him into her van. Poppy's kangaroo-pocket sweatshirt, handy for holding dog treats, celebrated the University of Michigan. She always dressed sensibly.

"Hey, did your Grand Rapids lady show up? I stopped in to see if you wanted a coffee from across the street."

Mary Ellen looked irritated. "She was here, said maybe five words, took the packet, and left. A very odd encounter."

"A packet?" Poppy looked puzzled. "I thought this was two groups playing Mah Jongg."

"It is a one-day tournament. But I invited the Grand Rapids group to come the night before, have a quick rules meeting, give people a chance to see Frankenmuth, and have a nice dinner together."

"So, the packet?" Poppy still looked confused.

"Times to meet, tournament rules, just basic information," Mary Ellen said defensively.

"Let's go across the street to the coffee shop and you can fill me in. I honestly thought this was a get-together to play a few rounds of Mah Jongg. I'm not sure I'm tournament ready," Poppy said. She played occasionally and enjoyed the social aspect of the game.

Mary Ellen grabbed her packet and purse, and the friends hurried across the always busy Main Street.

2: A Short Odyssey

Poppy's ostensibly white Odyssey minivan (it always needed a wash) was already parked crookedly, Poppy style, across the street by the coffee house in the public city lot located there.

CJ Bauer, a Frankenmuth police investigator, noticed the car and almost shivered, imagining fingernails scratching on now–extinct chalkboards. She had been looking for ages for some chance to ticket Poppy's car because it offended her sense of symmetry and civic spirit for someone to routinely and apparently without any conscience at all encroach on multiple parking spots at once.

While technically this was a privately owned lot, CJ had come to the conclusion that if, say, someone committed a more serious crime on that space, she would indeed investigate and give out tickets or make arrests. She decided she had been much too conservative in her interpretation of her jurisdiction over the situation. Perhaps a few parking tickets would help improve the parking skills of the best–known dog chaser in town.

She wheeled her marked police SUV in neatly, two spaces away from Poppy's car, pretty much as close as she dared park to it. She thought she spotted something odd sticking out from under the van, like a boot, maybe.

Her sense of order was even more highly offended. Had people become utterly brazen about dropping trash around, despite this town having more public trash cans per capita than any city in Michigan? That wasn't hyperbole. People kept such statistics. And CJ read them. Had Poppy simply taken to running over any sort of trash instead of parking beside it and toting it the four feet to the trash can at the sidewalk end of the parking lot? Her sense of disgust was palpable.

As she approached, her concern with Poppy's crooked parking gave way to the realization that there was a person under that van. Had Poppy finally run someone down? In public? In daylight and good weather? And no one knew or saw—or worse yet, cared? Even CJ was having a tough time with that quick scenario.

She picked up her radio and called for help—police and EMTs from the fire department. She lay down to get a better view, and sure enough, it was a woman, probably in her mid-fifties, unconscious—or worse. Had Poppy really gone and done it this time and killed someone? CJ actually hoped not. Although she'd love to give her a parking ticket or ten, she did have some regard for Poppy's work on a double homicide situation they'd had in town a few months back.

Lights and sirens quickly approached. Nothing in town was more than a couple minutes away at most from emergency vehicles, and the city kept up with their fleet, opting to purchase like-new ones with all the amenities vs. brand new, cheaper ones that left some things off.

Meantime, inside the coffee house and going over the Mah Jongg tournament packet, Mary Ellen and Poppy jumped up to realize the sirens were pulling into the parking lot not twenty feet from where they sat.

They rushed out the door, Poppy distressed to see her van within the circle of some event that had this much attention. "CJ!" hollered Poppy. "What's going on with my car?"

CJ redirected her attention fully on Poppy. "Poppy, there's a dead person under your car, and we need to figure out what happened. Did you have any sense of having run over, well, anything when you pulled in here?"

Poppy and Mary Ellen were both horrified. "Of course not!" said Poppy.

"Well, at the moment, Poppy, we just don't know what happened, and we're going to have to impound your car until we sort this all out. We are also going to need you to come over to the police station, please." Their eyes locked and they both knew that Poppy was beyond a doubt a suspect in something, although neither knew quite what.

EMTs had pulled the woman out from under the car and Mary Ellen took a good look. "Bootsie!" she shouted. "Poppy, it's Bootsie!" Bootsie herself remained staunchly and consistently unresponsive to Mary Ellen.

"Who's Bootsie?" Poppy and CJ both asked.

"Bootsie from Grand Rapids, who was going to have a team here to play at our Fischer Hall Mah Jongg tournament.

I just had a strange encounter with her, meeting her for the first time."

"So, if I have this right," CJ started, "Mary Ellen, you recently talked to our victim, and Poppy, it's up in the air if you ran over her with your mutt mobile." She was exasperated.

"Maybe she had a heart attack, like a normal tourist," said Ed, the chief of police. They hadn't noticed him make his appearance.

All three women turned and gave him a look.

"You missed what the scene looked like before the EMTs arrived," said CJ. "We've never had a tourist with a heart attack fall completely under a parked car before. We've got pictures, though."

Ed took out his ever-present Tums and took a handful.

3: Poppy Gets a Ride to the Police Station

Poppy wasn't cuffed or anything like that. She wasn't detained or arrested, but she glanced back mournfully, not so much at the dead body, which would have been a common reaction, perhaps, but at her beloved crooked car that they were getting ready to tow.

Ed said, "Poppy, we just need to record exactly what happened here, you know. It's not like we're going to print you and toss you in the holding cell." (In Ed's town, it was "the" holding cell. The police station wasn't big enough to have two of them.)

Yet, thought Poppy.

A few minutes later, Ed, CJ, and Poppy all sat in what was undeniably an interview room. Locks on the inside and outside, the TV-style one–way mirror/window, and a camera always on when the room was occupied. Ed had a mug of coffee—double–double cream—in front of him; Poppy had a tall glass of Keurig caramel vanilla latte—the best of bad choices, she thought, from the Keurig pile; and CJ had a bottle of water.

CJ started. "Poppy, you've got to understand—in fact, I'm positive you do understand—that it's rare to locate a dead body under a car that hasn't been run over. Can you take us back, second by second, to the act of parking your car?"

Poppy wrinkled her nose as CJ made finger quotes around the word "parking."

"Well, sure. Of course. But there was really a lot going on in the car at that time."

Ed and CJ both blinked.

Ed quietly said, "Well, you hadn't mentioned before anything 'going on' as you parked the car, so set the scene for us."

"Mary Ellen called me from Fischer Hall earlier to tell me that Munchie List was running around the parking lot in back of Fischer Hall. I figured it was time for a courtesy pickup, so I headed over."

This story was starting a lot earlier in the day than either Ed or CJ anticipated. Ed intervened because he couldn't stop himself. "What's a courtesy pickup, exactly?"

"Think of it like a ten-punch coffee card," said Poppy, all business now. "If I pick up your dog ten times, you ought to have a time when he gets a free ride home. This was Munchie's free ride."

"Are you telling me that you've actually picked Munchie up ten times?" said Ed, aghast.

"More like thirty," said Poppy.

CJ, trying to finally get to the parking lot with the body, said, "So you picked up Munchie and gave him a ride home. And then what?"

"Not exactly," said Poppy. "Munchie had trotted from the back of the Visitor and Welcome Center to the river area, nosing around. I had to go through the usual procedure of waving a hot dog around and calling him over. Meantime, I called Karen and told her I was grabbing Munchie for her—no charge—and could she meet me over at the Harvest parking lot and put him in her car. She was good with that. In fact, she hadn't noticed he had left the backyard somehow."

Ed and CJ sighed simultaneously. "Does this have anything to do with anything we are interested in, Poppy?" Ed was getting snappish, Poppy noticed, but she couldn't understand why.

"If you'd let me finish," she snapped back. "I had Munchie in the car, and had driven around and pulled into the parking lot from Main Street, noticing there seemed to be an available spot, when Karen pulled her car in from the back parking lot entrance, sending Munchie into a frenzy of … joy, I suppose, and excitement, definitely, seeing his mom in her own car. He was all over the place because I hadn't secured him. We were going such a short distance, and his ride was on the way. His tail was right in my face. I was trying to park very carefully, of course," Poppy continued, with a quick glance at CJ. "But I couldn't really see out the windshield, so I took my best guess and pulled into that spot."

"So," said Ed. "Sooo."

"So, what?" said Poppy. "So, I got out of the car, Karen grabbed Munchie, and I went into the coffee shop and ordered a drink. That's the whole story."

Ed and CJ were having an odd moment of mutual déjà vu. "So, Poppy, for the second time in a period of around a year there's somehow been you, a dead body, and Munchie in the same space at the same time. Doesn't that strike you as really weird?"

"Well, not really," said Poppy defensively. "All the other years before that, it never happened, so … it's still a very rare and unusual thing."

CJ got out of her chair, turned in a circle, and sat back down again. She and Ed were seeing what Poppy was missing—that indeed she might have run over or run down, or both, someone in the parking lot.

"Do you happen to know the woman named Bootsie who was found under your car?"

"No, Ed! Of course not!" said Poppy, as though that were a given in such a small town.

CJ tried to bring the temperature down. "We were hoping to quickly rule out that you ran over someone with your vehicle, but your version of events makes that harder rather than easier," she practically chirped, trying to keep the irritation out of her voice.

Poppy took a sip from her drink and considered that for a moment.

An officer knocked on the door and handed Ed a cell phone. "Here's a call for you, Chief, from the coroner's office."

Ed grabbed the phone. Adding to the sense of déjà vu was the fact it was Doc Adams again, moonlighting for the coroner's office. The county was still short of doctors doing autopsies. "Yes. Yes. Really? Ok, thanks. Let me know when you have all the results in, please."

Ed turned toward the women. "Poppy, you're off the hook. We still don't know how precisely a body made its way under your car, but we'll figure that out. But the one thing the doc knows for sure is that Bootsie's death wasn't due to being hit or run over by a car or anything else. We won't know what killed her until the lab results are complete."

"Great. Whew!" said Poppy. "Where are my car keys—and my car?"

"You'll get the car back when the techs have gone over it with a fine-tooth comb, Poppy. There could still be forensic evidence on the undercarriage, even if you didn't run her over. Someone will call you when we can release the car."

"Ok. Thanks." Poppy grabbed her phone and called Mary Ellen to get her out of there.

4: Reviewing the Events

Mary Ellen dropped Poppy off at her house and went home to share the events of the morning with her husband of many years, Todd. Todd tried to keep Mary Ellen from doing anything rash. In turn, he supported all her enterprises. It was a tricky balance.

"Todd, I'm home," Mary Ellen called as she walked in the front door. "I need to talk to you." Mary Ellen put her keys and purse down on the kitchen island as Todd walked toward her from the bedroom.

"I'm right here. I thought you were spending the morning organizing your Mah Jongg tournament. Are you finished already?"

Mary Ellen sighed and sat down on one of the chairs. "It's complicated." She then proceeded to fill Todd in on the morning's events: seeing Munchie, texting Poppy, meeting with Bootsie Van der Veer, and finding the dead body.

By the time she had finished, Todd was sitting next to her, shaking his head. "So where is Poppy now? Did she run over that lady?"

"CJ told me she was taking Poppy to the police station. The body was on its way to the morgue. Poppy doesn't think she hit anything or anybody, but she was distracted, as she had Munchie in the car with her. Karen was going to pick him up in the coffee shop parking lot."

"So, she might have hit this person?" Todd asked incredulously.

"She's a terrible parker and the car was crooked, as always, in the space. I thought she might have just parked over her, maybe. But the coroner's office called Ed and told him the body had not been run over at all. So they released Poppy and I dropped her off at her house. I don't know any more than that yet, other than that her car is being held for examination of possible evidence."

Todd shook his head. "So, we don't have to do anything drastic like bring Babycakes here? Great!"

Babycakes was Poppy's dog, whom she adopted from Midwest Boston Terrier Rescue. She had a terrible life before being taken in by the rescue. In return, Babycakes had helped Poppy adjust to life without her late husband, David. They were devoted to each other.

Todd grimaced. "I don't think that dog likes me."

Mary Ellen said, "What are you talking about? Dogs love you. We had Finnegan and Granby here over Christmas and you were their favorite person."

"Well, they are goofy golden retrievers. They like everyone. Babycakes always gives me the side-eye. You must have noticed it."

Just then, Mary Ellen's phone played "Who Let the Dogs Out."

"That's Poppy."

Mary Ellen picked up the phone. "Hey, are you ok?"

She listened briefly and picked up her purse and keys.

"Poppy wants to meet, and of course, still doesn't have her car. I'm going to run and get her. No worries about Babycakes needing to come here." She kissed his cheek and hurried out the door.

•••

"Let's go to the library and sit and talk in the quiet room. It's away from distractions and prying ears," said Mary Ellen when she picked up Poppy. Both of them ignored that it was called the quiet room because it was supposed to be silent. When no one else was using it, it was a great space for a two-person conversation.

Mary Ellen had been the head librarian at the Frankenmuth Wickson Library, and it was still one of her favorite places in town. The building was unique in that it had a gorgeous mural painted on the front by local artist Steve Hargash. In addition to the Mossner Room being designed for quiet study and privacy, it also had the most comfortable chairs.

"What happened at the police station?" asked Mary Ellen once they got settled. "We didn't have a chance to talk about it, really, on the way to your house earlier."

"I wasn't very helpful. The only person I saw this morning was you and, of course, Munchie. Ed wanted to know about cars I might have seen or strange events I might have witnessed. I told him I picked up Munchie behind Fischer Hall and parked over in the coffee shop parking lot after calling Karen to pick him up there. Then Karen picked up Munchie and moved him to her car, and I met you inside the Harvest as we had arranged. That's what happened and that's what I told Ed. Then CJ came in and gave Ed a note and I was told I could go."

"What did the note say?" Mary Ellen knew her friend had an idea about that note.

"Well, he didn't say exactly, but Doc Adams was sure Bootsie wasn't hit by any car. Our interview ended abruptly, and he said my car would be released after being examined for evidence. I'm hoping that happens today. I assume I didn't hit or run anyone over. I'm positive I would have noticed."

"Okay, so let's talk Mah Jongg for a minute. I've created a calendar of tournament events and times so we're all clear on what happens when, including gameplay, breaks, and players changing seats. It's going to be a great time!"

"Mary Ellen, that sounds too complicated. Will we be there until midnight?"

"No, Poppy, we'll play right along, minimal chitchat, because everyone knows how to play. It'll be quick work getting the last tables organized, but people will help with that."

"Mary Ellen, I'm a little concerned as to whether I am tournament-ready. How about I dish up the food? And what makes you so sure everyone knows what they're doing? We have a few rank beginners in the group."

"Poppy, you'll all be just fine."

5: THE FRIENDLY GAME

Poppy had agreed to meet a table of newbie players for a practice session before the Mah Jongg tournament, and that afternoon was the practice day. Heaven knows it had been a busy day, but they could still get their practice session in. They wouldn't be mixed with the experienced players at the actual tournament, it had finally been decided, but instead these players would find this a social learning experience. One of them would get a prize other than the usual table prizes. Poppy was a decent player, if not up to the level of Mary Ellen, and volunteered to help the beginners. They practiced at the Kaffee Haus, a popular location close to the library for coffee and lunch.

They had a full table—Poppy as mentor, Lisa, Nancy, and Beth—having pushed a couple small tables together. Poppy looked forward to answering questions and pointing out a few principles for them to bear in mind, even while playing the most casual game with each other.

"First," Poppy started, sounding a lot more like a drill sergeant than she imagined or intended, "remember the order of everything. There's no so-called fourteen-tile game at tournaments for those of you who have witnessed Florida play. The order is always pick, rack, throw. If you pick and know immediately that you're going to discard the tile you picked, it's fine to pick and throw. There seems to be some confusion about that. And tapping a tile on the table isn't racking it; in fact it doesn't have anything to do with the game, so someone could still call a discarded tile you wanted. If you're claiming a tile someone discarded, thus starting a turn for yourself wherever you are at the table, again it's call, rack on the flat part, add the remainder of tiles for your intended exposure, and discard." To brand new players, this might all sound confusing, but it shouldn't to anyone having played for a while.

"But what if you can't use it? Can you put the tile back in the discard pile you got it from?"

"Yes. But once you rack it, you own it."

"Well, if it's a friendly game, couldn't we remove it from our rack and put it back?"

"No. A friendly game is one where we all play by the rules."

Murmuring went around the table.

"What if it's a bad exposure and you're dead? Who will tell you that?"

"Anyone who notices," said Poppy, "and people are watching carefully what you expose to make sure it's a legitimate exposure. They might make a strategic choice to not mention it, but make sure you don't call yourself dead."

"So, what are you supposed to do if someone does call you dead?"

"Let's just play," said Poppy. "And promise me this. Everyone read the back of the card carefully multiple times—ten is not too many—before the tournament. Ok?"

She didn't wait for an answer, and started building her wall. Everyone else did the same. Lisa noted that there weren't enough tiles left for her to have thirty-eight in her wall. Poppy saw that Beth's tiles extended beyond her rack and pointed to those tiles and said, "Take two from there."

Beth was East in her position at the table and immediately pushed out her rack correctly, the right end of the wall extending diagonally toward the middle of the table. And then she picked four tiles from the wrong end of the wall. Nancy noticed and said, "Put those back! That's the wrong end of the wall!"

But too late. Beth had racked her four tiles already.

"Hey! You aren't supposed to rack those until we have them all!" said Lisa, upset.

Beth said, "Oh, sorry," and put them back onto the wall.

Poppy said, "There's no do-over on that, Beth. You've seen the tiles, and people having the wrong tiles completely changes the outcome of the game." With that, Poppy shoved her tiles from her wall in front of her into the middle.

"What? Wait!" shouted Nancy. "I just told her to put the tiles back. And even if she messed up her wall, there's nothing wrong with the rest of ours."

Customers and even baristas were starting to look over anxiously at the tones of voice of the four players, with Poppy being uncomfortable at the attention.

"I thought this was a friendly game!" said Lisa.

"What does that even mean?" hissed Poppy. "We are all going to humiliate ourselves in the tournament if we cannot even manage to pick our tiles. Look around! No one in this place knows how to play this game except maybe us, and we're still being stared at because they know things aren't right!"

"Well, Poppy," said Beth, every bit matching Poppy's hiss with her own, "honestly, when it comes to doing things properly, didn't you run down an out-of-town player, who is now dead, just yesterday? Someone named Bootsie?" The other three at the table, plus an accountant named Rudy and a couple more people having coffee at various tables, and Jonny the barista, sucked in their breath at this unfortunate question. Everyone in the room was wondering whether the hapless Bootsie had managed to be in that space before or after Poppy wheeled the Odyssey into the parking spot. Ed and CJ weren't the only people in town aware of Poppy's parking issue.

Poppy lowered her voice to a gritty whisper. "No. I did not run down anyone yesterday or any other day. Someone was under my car, and this is an investigation and nothing to be bandied about while trying to build our walls."

Poppy swept her eyes around the room, daring anyone to meet her gaze. Not one person came close. A couple of tourists, to the concern of the owner, grabbed their to-go cups and went.

The players hustled to build walls again, although in the excitement of tossing the tiles in the middle, the numbers didn't work out right and they were searching the floor for three missing tiles.

Rudy, used to hanging out with whoever might be having coffee, shouted out in a cheery auctioneer voice, "We have two tiles under our table!" He brought them over and asked where to put them. Poppy held out her hand to take possession of her tiles. The shop owner, Saren, sidled over and said, "Here's another one, Poppy, that slid over by the trash can."

"Thank you," she said stiffly. Poppy's right arm swept the table and once again collapsed all the walls into the middle.

There were more steps to master or at least complete before this hand officially started, and they finally managed to get through those, although everyone was now a bit afraid of Poppy and wondered when the fun part of the game would begin.

Twenty long, excruciating minutes later, the hand was over, Poppy had won, and she quickly declared practice done. These three were, after all, only going to play each other. No point getting picky. "Practice building walls so it feels automatic," she advised. "And show up for the tournament feeling relaxed, and in the mood to have fun. That's the most important part! Have a great time."

As Poppy went to the parking lot, her mind went back to the body under her car. She found parking tricky, but she wasn't a dangerous driver. How and why was Bootsie under her car? "I need to get home to Babycakes," Poppy said out loud to only herself. "I need to pat my dog and think."

She hopped in her freshly released from–the–impound Odyssey. The other three stood well back as Poppy reversed out of her spot, muttering to herself.

6: Who Is Bootsie?

CJ Bauer leaned into Ed Swartz's office. "Chief, I just logged into the DMV; a maroon 2021 Ford Edge is registered to a Bootsie Van der Veer. The address is 9854 River Road, Grand Rapids. The car has a personalized license plate, BOOT-Z. I imagine it is parked somewhere in Frankenmuth, as her last known encounter was inside Fischer Hall."

"Thanks, CJ. I'll let the patrol officers know to be on the lookout. The coroner just called. Bootsie probably hit her head on the parking curb. It appears her only injury is a caved-in skull consistent with hitting the concrete parking stop."

"Chief, is there any way Poppy could have parked over Bootsie's body? I mean, the woman cannot park that beast of a car she drives, so how could she possibly pull into a space with a body lying in it and miss it?"

"We had a chance to check the tires and there is no evidence that she ran over a body and no injuries on Bootsie that would indicate she had been run over."

CJ went back to her office to finish writing her report, as she was the officer first on the scene. CJ wrote very detailed reports so any officer working on the case would have few follow-up questions. She had just finished writing her final comments when Ed called from the hallway.

"CJ, Buddy found Bootsie's car. It was in the SpringHill parking lot. Let's go over there, talk to the front desk, and have the car towed."

Ed and CJ parked next to the car with the license plate BOOT-Z. They walked into the lobby of the SpringHill Suites.

"May we speak to the manager?" asked CJ.

"I'm the manager. May I help you?"

"We're from the Frankenmuth Police Department and we would like to have any information you have on a current guest, Bootsie Van der Veer."

Since both CJ and Ed were in uniform, and Kenzie, the manager, was from Frankenmuth, there was no need for badges and paperwork.

"Let me look." Kenzie pulled up customer information on her computer. "She checked in yesterday afternoon for a two-night stay. I checked her in. She was with a gentleman. Oh wait, really odd. His name was Van der Veer as well. But they took separate rooms."

Ed leaned on the counter. "Could you call his room to see if he's in? Ask him to meet us in the lobby if he is."

Ed and CJ walked over to a table on the other side of the empty lobby. He hoped to keep this conversation private. Kenzie called over to the police officers, "He'll be right down."

•••

A puzzled looking gentleman exited the elevator and headed for the front desk. Ed went over and intercepted him. "Mr. Van der Veer?"

"Yes. And you are?"

"I am Ed Swartz, Chief of the Frankenmuth Police Department. Could you come over here so we can talk privately?"

"What is this about? I have business to conduct. I'm on my way to an appointment."

"Please, have a seat." Ed steered him over to the table where CJ was sitting. "This is Detective CJ Bauer. Mr. Van der Veer, we have some difficult news to share. This morning a Bootsie Van der Veer suffered a fatal accident in town. Do you know Bootsie?"

"I'm Dennis, and yes, I know Bootsie. She is my wife, well, ex-wife. Bootsie? Dead? Are you sure? Good heavens, we had coffee together this morning. What happened?"

"Mr. Van der Veer, I'm sorry for your loss. It appears Bootsie fell and hit her head on a concrete parking curb. We're not sure of all the details, but we are treating her death as suspicious. You are divorced and yet you are at the same hotel. Can you explain your relationship?"

Dennis took a deep breath. "We own a business together. Van der Veer Electric. I do installation and Bootsie took care of the fixtures. We are a great team. Oh, were a great team."

CJ had been taking notes, and looked up. "You are based in Grand Rapids, but you are in Frankenmuth?"

"We have expanded our usual area. Building projects have slowed down, so we were looking at new locations to do business. We had a commercial job that would require both of us, and Bootsie had a residential opportunity to check out.

"She went to her client this morning, then she had to meet up with a Mah Jongg player. We were to go to the commercial property this afternoon."

CJ looked at Dennis. "She met with the Mah Jongg player, and do you know who her first appointment was with?"

"No, it was last minute, I think. She might have it written in her phone."

"Mr. Van der Veer, I'm going to have to ask you to officially identify Bootsie's body. Then I'll need to speak with you again. Here's the morgue's number in Saginaw. Please let me know your plans and please do not leave town."

"So, I'm stuck here, and I have to trek into Saginaw to identify the body? Oh, I'm sorry, that didn't come out right. I'm naturally upset. Of course, I want to help in any way I can."

"We'll be happy to take you to the morgue. Just let us know when you'll be going. Again, we are sorry for your loss."

As Ed and CJ walked to the police cruiser, Ed said, "He didn't seem terribly broken up, did he?"

"No," CJ looked back at the hotel. "Divorced, own a business together, and he didn't seem surprised either. I'll do some checking on Mr. Dennis Van der Veer."

7: Inheritance

Mary Ellen and Poppy walked into the Kaffee Haus together. They got the "regulars" treatment. Every barista could make their favorite drinks expertly. All they had to do was wave to Saren or one of the baristas and find a seat. Shortly after, two delicious and piping hot cappuccinos arrived at their table.

"So, Poppy, are you ready to fly to Baltimore tomorrow? Todd will pick you up at 8:00 a.m. We should get to the airport around nine thirty or so."

"Why are we leaving so early? Our flight isn't until noon."

Mary Ellen looked over her coffee cup. "Todd's flight leaves at 11:00 a.m., so we'll be at our gate early. So odd that we both are traveling on the same day to different places. He has a funeral to go to in Vermont for a cousin's wife. They all grew up together and have stayed in touch. I know it will be meaningful for Todd to be there.

"And we're going to pick up an antique Mah Jongg set that a very distant relative left to me. It is supposed to stay in the family, and I'm the oldest of the Hamilton family, so it's mine. I'm very excited, and the timing is perfect. I can display it at the tournament."

Poppy looked puzzled. "Can we play with it?"

Mary Ellen looked horrified. "Family legend says it is made of ivory. That makes it very rare and delicate. According to the attorney for the estate, there is documentation that identifies this set as acquired before 1947, so it is legal for me to have it. After that date, it became illegal to have any new ivory."

"Goodness." Poppy looked over at the counter. "There's Kenzie." Poppy waved, "Kenzie, when you get your coffee, can you join us for a minute?"

"Kenzie is going to dog-sit Babycakes while we're gone. I had hoped that Todd could watch her, but now he's not available."

Mary Ellen nodded and agreed that was too bad, but Kenzie would be great. She chose not to share that Todd and Babycakes had not really bonded. Poppy would be crushed. She couldn't imagine everyone didn't love Babycakes.

Kenzie sat down at the table. "Hello, Mrs. Freeman and Mrs. Lutz, how are you?"

"We're doing great, Kenzie." They were friends with Kenzie's mom and loved how polite she was. They had asked her several times to call them by their first names, but she wasn't comfortable with that yet. Neither had chalked it up to Kenzie thinking they were pretty old for first-name comfort.

"Kenzie, I'm going to be picked up at 8:00 a.m. tomorrow and will be back by dinnertime on Tuesday. Babycakes's food is in the bag under the counter. And her treats are on the shelf. The sheets in the master bedroom are clean, so please use that room. Babycakes will sleep right there. I have a booklet of how to take care of Babycakes that I'll put on the kitchen counter. I like for her to feel she's on her normal routine, you know. All of us like to feel that way."

"Mrs. Lutz, Babycakes and I will be fine. I can buzz over a few times during the day to let her out and play a little tug. The SpringHill isn't very busy right now during the week."

Mary Ellen asked, "How is the hotel manager training program going?"

"I really love it, and there is so much room for promotion; plus, it's never boring. We had a customer die—and her poor husband—or maybe her ex-husband— is still a guest. Chief Ed and CJ stopped in to ask him some questions."

Poppy grimaced. "It's not the lady who ended up under my car, is it?"

Kenzie looked confused. "You had a lady end up under your car? Did you run over her?"

"Why does everyone say that? I have never run over anyone, ever. "

Mary Ellen intervened. "Poppy, we all know you didn't run over anyone, but she was found dead under your car. People are bound to ask. Kenzie, so Bootsie has a husband or an ex who is in town? That's interesting. I imagine he's devastated."

"I really shouldn't talk about our guests."

"No worries, Kenzie. We were there when Chief Ed and CJ found the body. And Poppy has already been to the police station to try and explain the body-under-the-car situation."

Poppy looked unhappy. "And Mary Ellen actually knows Bootsie. They had a meeting at Fischer Hall the morning she was found dead. I would imagine that Ed and CJ will be chatting with Mary Ellen soon."

Mary Ellen and Poppy had been friends and business partners long enough to tease each other in such a way. Kenzie looked a little concerned and stood up to leave. "I'm going to work. Mrs. Lutz, I'll see you in the morning. Have a good trip, Mrs. Freeman."

"This whole body-under-the-car thing is going to set Kenzie back in using our first names by five years," muttered Poppy. "We scared her off. But you know we are connected to this case. I'm surprised that Ed and CJ have not called you in, Mary Ellen. After all, you met Bootsie and were the reason she was in town."

"Poppy, that's not true. She told me she was here on business—she was in the lighting business, and her husband is here as well. After we get back from our trip, we'll stop in and talk to Ed. He'll want to hear our thoughts."

8: When It's Too Easy

Poppy stopped home after coffee, wanting to get her paperwork organized before anything else. She worried that her tax records took on a similar appearance to her car, even though her home generally was organized and clean. Knowing that tax people appreciated information in categories and temporal order, she thought she'd get a head start.

When she pulled into her driveway, however, she was completely baffled to see the one, the only, the infamous Chuckie peeking out from behind a bush near her front door. And she hadn't even been looking for him. It was like he was on the loose and volunteering to be caught. This is entirely too easy, she thought.

Chuckie, for the few who didn't know him, was a small Maltese mix with a giant attitude. He had a small-guy complex and didn't hesitate to bite when it seemed the best defense. He seemed to have only one true attachment in the world—his own kid, Marcia, who was in third grade—and Chuckie often went looking for her.

"What the heck, Chuckie?" muttered Poppy. It was normally not a good thing to have dogs behaving out of character. The second out–of–character dog, noticed Poppy, was her own Babycakes, the Boston terrier, who was looking down at the small Chuckie from her window–seat perch, not barking, not pacing, just staring in surprise. And what else was it Poppy saw on Babycakes's face? Could it be concern? It sure looked like it.

Poppy left the car in the driveway and came around front to take a look at Chuckie, cooing soft words. "Hi, Chuckie! Whatcha doing here?"

Chuckie didn't meet her eyes in his normally defiant way. He knew he was on someone else's turf and wasn't comfortable at all. In fact, he was shaking. He glanced up at Babycakes staring down and started shaking harder.

"Chuckie, this is your lucky day!" said Poppy soothingly. "I'm giving free rides today, it appears. And Munchie is already home. I can give you a ride so that you can hang out with Marcia!"

At the sound of Marcia's name, Chuckie made brief eye contact with Poppy and quickly looked down again, crying a little.

When Poppy held out her arms, Chuckie advanced and let her pick him up without protest. "Wow," said Poppy. "Something's terribly wrong. We need to go to your house and see what's up."

She set Chuckie gently in the back seat and watched in amazement as he snuffled around actually looking for something to eat. "It's your lucky day, Chuckie! There's a little prosciutto back there from a leftover charcuterie order at Prost that I snagged on the way out the door the other night." Chuckie quickly located it and started eating like he hadn't eaten in a while. Poppy knew something was radically wrong and called CJ to see if she might meet them at Chuckie's house.

"Sure, Poppy, but what do you think's going on?"

"I don't know, but something is very wrong with this dog, and I'm about to wander into a situation that might be … strange."

"I'm on my way," said CJ.

Meantime, CJ was thinking, at least as far as she or Poppy knew, there was nobody under her van.

•••

Poppy and CJ pulled into Chuckie's people's driveway about the same time. The grass hadn't been cut for a good couple of weeks. Blinds were down. A window on the front door was broken. The gate of the wrought iron security fence that surrounded the property hung open, a security-code box lying on the ground close to the gate. It seemed to CJ that was a lot of fence to secure one small dog, no matter how badly he wanted to be with Marcia.

CJ called over to Poppy to stay in her van, and she called for backup.

Ed and two patrolmen showed up in short order, the trip from the police station being no more than a mile and a half to Chuckie's house in an especially pricey development. But the house was on a private cul-de-sac where others hadn't been built yet and therefore the situation could easily go unnoticed by neighbors, open gate and all.

After a quick walk around the house, the police found that the front door was indeed accessible and walked into the house, two heading in one direction, two in the other.

After a moment, CJ called, "In here!" from what turned out to be the master bedroom. Lying on the floor was Terri, Marcia's mother—the one afraid of her own dog, Poppy recalled from previous encounters, who of course didn't stay in her van. She was right behind the police, holding a quiet Chuckie.

Poppy let out a squeak of "Holy crap!" as she noticed that Terri had been stabbed.

Ed startled at the sound of Poppy's voice and turned to her. "Poppy, great call to get us out here; now please take the dog and wait in your van while we secure the crime scene."

Poppy had a brief thought about the two murders in Frankenmuth several months ago and wondered what was going on here. Where was Marcia? Where was Jack, Terri's husband? And who on the planet would take the little oddball one–person Chuckie? She retreated to her car.

Ed and CJ started the process of taking photos of the crime scene and the state of the house. Crime scene technicians were on their way and would preserve the scene in other ways. There had clearly been a struggle, and Terri was on the losing end.

9: What Did Happen to Bootsie?

Poppy and CJ made short work of giving Chuckie some unfamiliar security. "I grew up with dogs, Poppy," CJ told her. "Granted, they were shepherds and border collies, but all dogs tend to do well with predictability and a clear understanding of what the expectations are—both from people and toward people. This little guy is a hot mess of instability. I can foster him and give him some security and training if you'd like."

Poppy looked at CJ over her desk thunderstruck. She had anticipated having to talk CJ into exactly this. Even Poppy was always impressed that CJ was clear in her behavioral expectations, of people anyway. Poppy was so grateful and happy that Chuckie could go home with CJ that she vowed (only to herself—no point going crazy here) to do a better job of parking her car and reducing one of CJ's irritants in her life. One reason Poppy wasn't going to say anything out loud was that she really did think her parking was fine. But she decided she'd take some pictures and see if she could figure out what it was that so irritated CJ.

Just while both women were absorbing CJ's newfound foster-mom status, Ed walked in with a folder and a puzzled look on his face.

"What's going on here, you two? Or is it you three?" he said, acknowledging the ball of fluff sitting on CJ's lap growling at him. "Does he have to growl at me? That seems antisocial."

CJ piped in, "Never correct a dog for growling, Ed. A growl stands between you and a bite."

"What the hell? What are you talking about? Well, we can get into that later. I have here the coroner's report that gives us more information but doesn't shed a lot of light on the story of what happened," said Ed.

"Can I stay and hear this?" said Poppy. "I feel with one body under my car, and then another body CJ and I discovered, that I'm a part of this already."

Ed didn't exactly invite her to stay so much as he failed to kick her out, which was good enough for Poppy. She knew a passive invitation when she heard it.

"Well, of course, there was no trauma to the body like one would expect had Bootsie been either intentionally struck or even accidentally run over by a vehicle. We have, though, a cause of death but not a means of death."

CJ and Poppy both knew that the cause was what killed her, and the means of death was how she met her fate—accident, illness, murder, things like that.

Both women stared at Ed, awaiting more information. Even Chuckie had a rare moment of focus and was no longer growling.

"The cause of death is simple enough. She died of heart failure due to an extreme overdose of caffeine."

Ed paused as the women took this in.

CJ jumped in. "What do you think this means, Ed?"

"Well, there are at least three possibilities. Bootsie either knowingly and intentionally overdosed on caffeine in some form, either accidentally or intentionally taking her own life. Or she unwittingly took a huge overdose of caffeine delivered with an intent to kill her, or, in my opinion, the least likely thing—someone gave her the caffeine but not with intent to harm her."

Poppy noted, "That leaves a lot of possibilities." The four of them sat in silence for a good thirty seconds, each mulling this over (except Chuckie, of course, but who knows).

"How does this shed light on why she was under my car?" asked Poppy.

Ed and CJ together said, "It doesn't."

10: Travels with Poppy and Mary Ellen

Promptly at 8:00 a.m., Todd pulled into Poppy's driveway. Poppy was on the front porch. She waved goodbye to Babycakes and Kenzie, who were in the front window, and opened the back door of the car to hop in.

"Mary Ellen, why are you in the back seat?"

Mary Ellen grinned. "Todd thought we'd enjoy chatting side by side instead of me having to turn around to talk. Plus, this way he doesn't have to join in, but he can drive and listen to Sirius."

"Good, I called you last night, but you didn't answer. I stumbled upon another murder."

Mary Ellen leaned forward. "Stumbled? Poppy, what does that mean?"

Poppy took a breath. "It was odd. Chuckie turned up in my yard yesterday afternoon. You know how he is usually very unfriendly."

"Unfriendly? As in, he bites anyone who tries to pick him up?"

"Well, he was shaking, and let me pick him up without the Chuckie gloves. So, I planned on taking him home, and he was acting so oddly, I gave CJ a call to meet me there. Mrs. Mills has never been all that happy to see me or Chuckie. When we got to the house, the security gate was open. It didn't look like anyone had been there for a while. CJ told me to wait in the car while she called for backup. When the boys arrived, I followed them into the house."

Todd said, "Poppy, a law enforcement officer told you to wait in the car. What were you thinking?"

"I was thinking I'd wait until the other officers showed up. Anyway, Mary Ellen, that house is not dilapidated inside. There was no furniture, but the hardwood floors were beautiful, the wood trim expensive. The inside does not match the outside at all. We all split up once we were inside. I walked down a short hallway to the master bedroom. There on the floor was a body, and lots of blood. CJ turned around and ordered me out of the house. We have another murder!"

Mary Ellen gasped. "Did you recognize the body? Did you see her?"

"Like I said, I was immediately dismissed. But I have delivered Chuckie to that house before and met this lady. It's Chuckie's mom."

•••

Traffic moved along and they arrived at the airport by nine forty-five. Todd found a parking place in the garage that was not close to the door. It wasn't terribly inconvenient since everyone was carrying their bags on. As they walked to the terminal, Poppy stopped for a moment. "Barney? Barney? Is that you?"

Mary Ellen and Todd slowed down. Mary Ellen looked behind Barney. "CJ? Is that you?"

Barney and CJ looked sheepishly at the threesome. Todd interrupted, "Barney, good to see you again, and CJ as well. I have to run. I have a plane to catch. Mary Ellen, I'll see you tomorrow at the arrival/departure board. Poppy, have a good flight. Watch out for ME."

Mary Ellen gave Todd a quick kiss and then turned her attention to this unusual situation. Poppy was asking Barney where he had been and where he was going. Barney explained, "I'm just back from Africa. My law firm had an international case that was being tried in Kenya. CJ offered to pick me up. I thought I'd spend a few days in Frankenmuth. I'm sorry you won't be there."

Mary Ellen looked at CJ, who was not making eye contact with anyone. "Fortunately, we're just going to Baltimore, Maryland, for the day. We'll be back tomorrow."

Barney, who did look tired, said, "I'll need today and tonight to recharge. I'm spending the night at the SpringHill so I can sleep and not bother anyone. Let's plan on dinner tomorrow night."

Quick hugs were exchanged, and Barney and CJ hurried off. Poppy and Mary Ellen walked toward the terminal. "Umm, wow, that was odd," said Mary Ellen.

"I know, what are the odds of running into Barney at the airport?" Poppy shook her head.

"No, I mean CJ and Barney. That was odd. Here's PreCheck—you go first." Mary Ellen let Poppy walk in front of her.

Poppy had her boarding pass out and handed it to the

TSA agent. "Ma'am, you are not PreCheck. Return to the concourse, and the next left is the line you need."

Mary Ellen looked at her friend. "You are not PreCheck? I never thought to ask. I'll meet you on the other side." She handed her boarding pass to the agent and entered the screening area.

Poppy found the entrance to the regular screening area and a long line. She patiently waited for her turn. Since David's death she hadn't done much traveling by plane. She discovered not much had changed, just the number of people traveling. She grabbed a bin, threw her backpack into it, and waited to go through the metal detector. A TSA agent yelled, "You must remove your shoes; phones and quart bags must be placed in the bin with your carry-on." Poppy got a little flustered. Her shoes were sneakers and she had to bend down to untie them. Then she had to pick them up and put them in the bin, except her bin had rolled into the machine. She then decided that a good option was to carry her shoes through the metal detector.

"Madam," an imposing TSA agent said, "shoes go in a bin." He grabbed a bin from behind the screener and told Poppy to place the shoes on the belt. Poppy did as she was told and walked back to go through the detector.

Poppy could see Mary Ellen sitting in a chair waiting for her. They exchanged a wave. Just then a loud buzzer went off. Poppy turned around to see her backpack being held up. "Whose backpack is this?" Poppy reluctantly raised her hand.

A TSA agent led her to a table and asked her to unpack her backpack. Poppy pulled out her clothes for the next day, a book she was reading, a dog leash, a water bottle, and a small pouch. She looked at the agent. "First, you cannot bring liquids through screening." He threw out the water bottle.

By this time Mary Ellen had come over to the table to see what was holding things up. "Poppy, is everything ok?"

The agent had just reached for the pouch that was on the table. He opened it and poured the contents out. There was a pocketknife, a small wire cutter, a bottle of unmarked medicine, and a dog whistle. He looked at Poppy. "Ma'am?"

Poppy looked at him. "I'm a dog catcher. Those are things that help me. Dogs sometimes get caught up in stuff that needs to be cut off. I assure you I am a respectable citizen."

Mary Ellen looked at the agent. "Confiscate it all. She can replace it. It was an accident that she left it in her work backpack. We are so sorry, aren't we, Poppy?" Mary Ellen gave her a poke in the back.

"Yes, I am sorry. I'll just grab my shoes, and my phone. Can we go?" Poppy did not sound at all remorseful, but the agent decided that they were not a risk to the public. All of Poppy's tools were tossed in a garbage can.

Poppy found a chair to put on her shoes. Mary Ellen stood next to her. "Why did you tell them to throw out my tools?"

"So we could get on the plane. You know things like knives are not allowed."

Poppy looked a little embarrassed. "I totally forgot that pouch was in there. How far to our gate?"

"Not far, and we can use the moving walkway. It really makes getting to gates so much easier."

The girls went down the escalator to the main concourse. Gate 60 was not a long walk. As Poppy started to look for a seat, she noticed Mary Ellen going past their gate. "Mary Ellen—it's right here."

Mary Ellen turned around. "I'm going to get a drink."

"Good thought. I'll have a water."

"I'm having a drink drink. There's a bar next door. Let's grab a seat and chat."

Poppy sat down at the bar next to Mary Ellen. "It's ten thirty in the morning. Did you have breakfast? They don't allow drunks on planes. Mary Ellen? Is this wise?"

"I do not like to fly. I don't like takeoff, I don't like turbulence, I don't like landing. I don't like sitting in a silver tube rocketing across the sky. But a glass of wine or two makes it tolerable." Mary Ellen was very definite.

"I'll have a Sauvignon Blanc, please—a fourteen ounce. Thank you."

"Mary Ellen, that's a lot of wine. Oh, this is not a good idea. We need to be at our gate so we can hear our flight information."

"They won't announce anything for at least forty-five minutes. We will not miss our flight. I promise. I'm looking forward to seeing this Mah Jongg set. You're sure you don't want a drink?"

11: THE HAMILTON ESTATE

Mary Ellen and Poppy took an Uber to Margaret Hoffman née Hamilton's attorney's office. The address they gave the Uber driver happened to take them to the Inner Harbor, a beautiful area designed for tourists, businesses, and the local sports teams. The attorney's offices were in a newer building not far from the Baltimore Convention Center. The girls checked the directory in the lobby and took the elevator to the twelfth floor. Jane Gross's office was right across from them as they got out of the elevator.

"Ladies, please come right in. I'm Jane Gross, and you must be Mary Ellen Freeman?" A petite blond dressed in a beautifully cut green suit stood by a door that appeared to open into another office. "My assistant just stepped out. I wanted to greet you personally."

"Thank you, Ms. Gross. I'm Mary Ellen Freeman, and this is my friend Poppy Lutz." They met Jane halfway and shook hands.

"Please call me Jane. Come in and have a seat. May I offer you water or coffee?"

"No, thank you." Mary Ellen and Poppy both laughed, as they had answered together.

"Well, thank you for coming. I enjoyed knowing Margaret. Did you know her?"

Mary Ellen volunteered some background. "I knew of her, but we never met. Our family was small, but no one kept in touch. I did some family research a few years ago and corresponded with her briefly. I wish I had followed up and arranged a get-together."

"She was an amazing woman. She was a librarian at the Milton S. Eisenhower Library at Johns Hopkins University for years. It is one of the premier research libraries in the country."

Mary Ellen gasped. "I was a librarian as well. My goodness, she never mentioned it."

"I wonder if that's why she left you this family heirloom?" Jane pointed to the intricate box that was on her desk. "Would you like to see it?"

"Oh my, yes. In your letter you said it was an old Mah Jongg set. I am an avid player, so I am very excited to own not just a beautiful set of tiles, but tiles that have a personal connection."

Jane opened the lid of the box. Inside was an exquisite set of Mah Jongg tiles. They were an ivory color with familiar markings. Mary Ellen assumed they were a Chinese set and would need some modifications to be played American style.

"As I wrote you, they are made of ivory. Margaret had that confirmed a few years ago. She has also included a brief history of your family and how they came to her."

Mary Ellen was still staring at the set. Poppy nudged her. "Oh, how thoughtful of her."

"Being a research librarian had its advantages. Let me get this paperwork signed and you and Poppy can get to your hotel and maybe have time to explore our city. I would suggest that you leave the set in the hotel safe. It is valuable and irreplaceable."

Mary Ellen quickly signed some papers. She and Poppy got up and thanked Jane. On their way out, they noticed that Jane's assistant had returned. She was a woman about their age and looked very much like Jane. As they left, they heard Jane call her "Mom".

"I like that attorney. She's interesting and employs her mom. Can you imagine if we worked for our kids?" Both of them rolled their eyes.

The hotel was right around the corner so there was no need for a cab. They were still carrying their luggage. Mary Ellen had tucked the Mah Jongg set into her carry-on, which made for an easier walk.

After checking in and securing the treasure in the hotel safe, they went out to do some exploring.

"When are you going to read the letter Margaret wrote about your inheritance?"

"I'll read it over cocktails when we get back to the hotel. We really don't have much sunlight and it is getting cooler. Shall we just stroll around?" asked Mary Ellen.

"Or we could go on a dragon boat. I have never been on one, and they look like so much fun. Let's do it!"

Mary Ellen smiled. That was why she enjoyed Poppy. She was up for anything.

●●●

Mary Ellen and Poppy sat in the lobby bar, each with a glass of wine. Mary Ellen pulled out a handwritten letter from her relative Margaret. "She has beautiful handwriting. How old-school to handwrite a letter."

Poppy leaned in to inspect the writing. "Read it! I'm anxious to hear how that magnificent set came to you."

Dear Freeman family,

This Mah Jongg set has been in the Hamilton family since the early 1850s. The original Hamilton brothers came from Scotland to Canada in 1845. Two of the brothers went to the United States, but Thomas stayed in Canada. He is the Hamilton who I am descended from. In 1867 the Canadian government was encouraging people to move to western Canada. Thomas was single and looking to make some money. In the late 1850s Chinese immigrants came to Canada for cheap labor and the gold rush. Thomas met a Chinese woman, Mei. Her family did not approve of her relationship with Thomas and disowned her. Sadly, no one approved of their relationship, so Thomas decided to move to upstate New York, where his brothers had settled. This Mah Jongg set belonged to Mei; it was one of the few things from her culture that she had.

The set has been passed down to the oldest child of each generation. Enclosed, find the appropriate wills that mention the Chinese box. My father, Kenneth, who moved to Baltimore after WW2, referred to it in his will as a Chinese tea box. Since I never saw it in my childhood home, I assume it was stored *in the attic. Imagine my surprise and delight to find an ivory Mah Jongg set.*

Hopefully you will appreciate this piece of our shared family history.

Sincerely,

Margaret Hoffman

Mary Ellen folded the letter and returned it to the envelope. "What a wonderful surprise. I'm so excited to share it at the tournament this week. The players will be amazed."

"Do you know how much it's worth? Should you insure it? That seems risky, Mary Ellen."

"Well, that's a good point, the insurance. I'll have Todd investigate that. But no one at a Mah Jongg tournament is going to steal an old Mah Jongg set."

Poppy nodded. "Let's finish our wine and grab a bite to eat. We must be at the airport early since that TSA thing takes forever. I assume you will need a glass of courage, even though it will be 8:00 a.m.?"

Mary Ellen gave Poppy a withering look, then smiled and said, "Yes, my dear, I think I will have a sip before boarding. Thanks for reminding me."

12: Barney Meets Dennis

All the articles Barney had read about jet lag and all the advice given him had helped him develop his own routine. He slept when tired, ate when hungry, and exercised and did work when awake, no matter the time on the clock. He eventually adjusted to the current time zone. This made him a terrible house guest. Barney had planned on contacting Poppy after his adjustment phase was over. The SpringHill was the perfect place. After his arrival at 10:30 a.m., he went to the Kaffee Haus and ordered a sandwich. His room was available early, so he checked in and lay down for an hour. After a shower and fresh clothes, Barney was ready for a walk around town.

Frankenmuth was a great walking town. The new Frankenmuth River Walk was exactly as named, a delightful walk along the river. It suited Barney's mission to have a quiet walk with river noises and views. The path ended in the parking lot behind Klaus the Maus, who guarded the front door of the Cheese Haus. Barney finished his walk and went across the street to the SpringHill.

The lobby was quiet. Barney asked at the front desk for a bottle of water and decided to sit and read the Frankenmuth News before the next nap. He had just opened the paper, when in walked Chief Ed Swartz. Ed stopped at the front desk and talked to the hotel manager. Barney knew Ed from a murder case last year that involved a client and a carriage driver. Poppy and Mary Ellen had helped Ed and CJ bring the killer to justice. It was a tricky case with a wild and unexpected ending.

"Ed," Barney stood up to shake hands, "how are you? Any new cases to solve?"

Ed walked over and shook Barney's hand. "Hi, Barney! Are you in town for a client or a vacation?"

The elevator doors opened, and an angry looking man stepped into the lobby. "Finally! Are you here to tell me I can go home? I have a business to run, and while I'm sad Bootsie is dead, I have my job and hers to complete. I had nothing to do with her death. I need to go home. Who are you?" The man stared at Barney.

"I'm Barney Mead. And you are?"

"I'm Dennis Van der Veer, and I'm innocent. My wife died; she met with a Mah Jongg lady and died, under a car. I seem to be a suspect. It seems like the Mah Jongg person, or the car driver, should be prime suspects."

Barney tilted his head and looked at Ed. "Can I jump to the conclusion that ..."

Ed shook his head. "Mr. Van der Veer, if we could have a few words in private. This won't take long."

"Ed, I'll leave you to it. I'm headed upstairs. Mr. Van der Veer, I'm sorry for your loss."

Ed sat down and motioned for Dennis to sit as well. "Mr. Van der Veer, I just wanted to inform you that we will be taking Mrs. Van der Veer's car into police possession to see if there is any information to help solve her murder. We will need you to sign this release. I am hopeful that we can allow you to go home in the very near future. Thank you for your cooperation."

Dennis signed the release and stalked to the elevator. "I want a full report by tomorrow. And I do need to go home." He got on the elevator and stared ahead as the door closed.

Ed got up and called the office. "You can pick up the Van der Veer car. I have the release."

13: What's Up with Barney?

Todd met Mary Ellen and Poppy at the gate. As no one had checked luggage, they were able to go right to the car. Todd pulled out of the airport and started telling Mary Ellen about his trip. Poppy tuned most of the conversation out as they were talking about family who Poppy had never met. She was thinking about the body that was found under her car and making a mental note to visit with Ed and CJ when they got back.

Todd looked at Poppy in the rearview mirror. "What was the deal with Barney?"

Poppy looked confused. "Barney?"

"Remember, we saw him in the airport garage with CJ? What was that about?" Poppy pulled out her phone. "Let me text him."

"BARNEY, WE ARE DRIVING BACK FROM THE AIRPORT. WOULD YOU LIKE TO STAY AT MY HOUSE? UNLESS YOU HAVE OTHER PLANS?"

"WELCOME BACK. I WOULD
LOVE TO STAY WITH YOU AND
HANG OUT WITH BABYCAKES.
THANKS FOR ASKING."

"WE SHOULD BE HOME IN
ABOUT AN HOUR. I ASSUME
YOU DON'T HAVE A CAR?"

"NO, BUT I AM PLANNING ON
RENTING ONE. CAN I UBER TO
YOUR HOUSE THIS EVENING?"

"OR CJ COULD BRING YOU? WE
DON'T HAVE UBER IN
FRANKENMUTH. OR I COULD SWING
BY AND PICK YOU UP?"

"DO YOU HAVE YOUR CAR? DID
THE POLICE TAKE IT? DIDN'T YOU RUN
OVER SOMEONE?"

Poppy put her phone down on the seat and yelled, "I did
not run over anyone! Barney seems to have heard that
ridiculous story. Why would anyone think that?"

"Because a body was found under your car," Todd said.
"Poppy, it's not too much of a leap to conclude you ran
over someone. Now, we know it's not true. Let the facts
come out in the police report." Mary Ellen couldn't talk
because she was laughing too hard.

"I'LL PICK YOU UP AT 5. WHERE ARE
YOU STAYING?"

"AT THE SPRINGHILL. THANKS,
POPPY. SEE YOU THEN."

At five o'clock, Poppy pulled up in front of the SpringHill Suites. Barney was waiting with a suitcase and a few bags.

"Hi, Poppy. Thanks so much for the offer. I grabbed some wine and cheese from the Cheese Haus and a charcuterie board from Prost. Will that do for dinner tonight? You must be tired from traveling."

"Barney, thank you. Sounds great. Let's go and give Babycakes a very pleasant surprise."

Over glasses of wine and a table full of meats, cheeses, and spreads, the two friends caught up. Barney had been in Africa for a trial involving the illegal ivory trade. The Swiss organization he worked for provided legal assistance to Kenya and other countries with elephant populations to prosecute poachers. Poppy told him about Mary Ellen's newly acquired ivory Mah Jongg set.

Before Barney could explain the background of the trial, Poppy looked at him, "So, CJ? What's the story there?"

"No real story. We ran into each other in Chicago a few months ago. She used to live there, and I've attended many seminars there over the years. We talked about favorite restaurants. She's a nice person. Listen, I'm exhausted. I'm going to go to bed. Babycakes, are you coming with me?"

Babycakes looked soulfully at Poppy and trotted right after Barney. Poppy huffed, picked up the last of the food, and settled in to watch *Midsomer Murders* before bed.

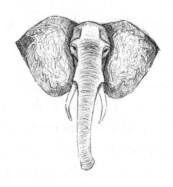

14: Five Years Ago: Barney in Nairobi

After a long haul in business class (Detroit to Amsterdam to Nairobi), the plane touched down at Jomo, the major Kenyan airport. Barney was contemplating the trip just before this one to Geneva, where he had been offered some interesting (but not full time) work for the World Wildlife Fund. The customs line at Jomo was slow today. Maybe that was normal.

Barney went all-in for his clients, in this case potentially the World Wildlife Fund. He wanted to take a look at protected wildlife in one of the countries with a huge diversity of species and see what he could do from a law enforcement angle. How could the country put donated money to use? And how could money raised cut off the demand for illegal products like ivory?

He wouldn't be in Kenya long. That night he was staying in an upscale, fully staffed rental home and planned to sleep off the trip. Tomorrow he would go on a day safari. Since it was in Nairobi National Park, he wouldn't see elephants, but he'd see a lot of other animals. The next day he'd be touring the Sheldrick elephant orphanage and then flying out that night to Geneva for another conversation with the World Wildlife people.

A waiting driver picked him up, and in less than two hours, he was settled outdoors with a drink in his hand and a plate of appetizers, taking in the plants and animals around the large yard. He was jarred to see a couple of baboons flying past him, one helping himself to a handful of appetizers that was quickly replaced. As slow as the baboons were fast, a warthog wandered past him, headed who knows where at his own unconcerned pace. He apparently sometimes stopped for a break.

Just around dusk, as he dozed off on the patio, he heard a sound that made his every hair stand on end. The sound of a roaring African lion, probably three miles away but seeming much closer, pierced the night. Barney had a feeling he didn't quite recognize, and he contemplated that he was hearing a free beast, one not in a cage, not fed by a zookeeper, not roaring like the captive lion in Pat Conroy's famous scenes in *Lords of Discipline*, not provided with a mate for breeding—but a hungry killing machine who was no doubt going on the hunt that very night as nature intended. He finally realized that feeling was atavistic—new to him, no matter how ancient. Who knew it still survived in human nature?

The next day was amazing. Lions, wildebeests, hyenas that were much larger and spookier to encounter than the ones he might have seen on TV, ostriches prancing on their way to a drink, hippos in the river (according to the guides, they might look goofy but were seriously dangerous), and zebras, gazelles, and giraffes dotting the whole landscape.

The guide stopped by the famous Ivory Burning Site, where the ashes of elephant and rhino ivory were burned by the government to take the profit out of slaughtering and reducing the population of these increasingly rare animals. The first twelve-ton burning was in 1989 and the last was in 2016. A monument remained for visitors to contemplate.

He was lucky enough to see a famous group of white rhinos, as well as endangered black ones, in the bush. The day ended on a perfect note. The guides were excited to point out, on the edge of a tree line, the most elusive big cat, a leopard. They were solitary creatures and avoided contact with pretty much everyone. On safari, they were a photographer's dream. Barney was no exception as his camera clicked full speed.

His last morning in Kenya, elephants were on full display at Sheldrick's orphanage. Of course, the need for an orphanage was caused by poaching. And poaching was caused by the insatiable drive of humans to dominate and use rather than coexist with other species.

Barney had a soft touch for animals, from family dogs to elephants. He could find some time to help this cause, he thought, and there were multiple ways he might be useful, he decided as he boarded the plane for Geneva and eventually home. His work would be in his own country, he was assured.

By the time he met up with the Feds in Frankenmuth five years later, he was no stranger to undercover work. He himself was amazed that all this brought him back again to Frankenmuth.

15: The Intervention

Poppy and Mary Ellen had decided to meet in one of the new conference rooms over at the library for a work session. The rooms were bright and pretty much soundproofed, and a treat to work in.

Poppy noticed Mary Ellen's convertible parked in the library's lot and thought that she was likely doing a little browsing through the latest new books on display before their meeting. But when she walked in and looked around, she didn't see her. Michelle caught her eye and pointed upstairs where the conference rooms were located. They were fishbowl rooms with glass walls. People may not have been able to hear anyone in there, but they could certainly see them.

Poppy was shocked to find not just Mary Ellen there but also Ed, CJ, and even Todd and Barney. Had some disaster happened she hadn't heard about yet? Were they really going to have a brainstorming session on the two recent murders? (Although it wouldn't be the usual police response to invite this particular group to help them solve crimes and meet at the public library.)

As Poppy entered the room, she couldn't help but notice that Ed, CJ, Mary Ellen, and even Todd muttered hi but weren't really making the direct eye contact that all those people were noted for. Indeed, only the unflinching lawyer, Barney, greeted her with a warm hello and commented that he saved her a seat by him.

She glanced at Barney, sat down, and got to the point. "What's up here? It's not my birthday."

Everyone looked at Ed, who cleared his throat. "Hey, Poppy! I picked up your favorite drink from the Kaffee Haus, and you know what? They knew exactly what you'd want."

"For Pete's sake, Ed, you sound like a moron. What's this all about?" Poppy ungratefully exclaimed. "Is Barney here to protect my rights?"

Barney leaped right in. He was the only one of the bunch on the side of the angels. "I'd be lying to deny that, Poppy. But relax. No one's going to be arrested unless you're mad enough to break glass walls." No one laughed.

CJ couldn't stand it any longer. She plunged ahead. "Poppy, we've looked at the situation of Bootsie under your car—and we're all glad she's dead of something other than being crushed by the mutt mobile."

Ed literally slapped his forehead at this.

"And we've reviewed your statement about, as you put it, 'a lot going on' in your car as you were parking it."

"And?" said Poppy. "You think she died of exhaust fumes?"

"No, no, no. We know she died of caffeine poisoning," Ed hustled along in his explanation.

"Exactly. Like a bad joke," said Poppy.

"And Todd, what on earth are you doing in this meeting? I'm always glad to see you, but I'm not sure why you're here, unless you're going to confess to something," said Poppy sarcastically.

Todd responded, "I'm only confessing to providing a little support to Mary Ellen since she's semi-afraid of offending you over all this." He pulled out a cigar, looked around, and put it away again. He needed to walk, he thought. Mary Ellen could handle this.

"Look," said Mary Ellen. "There's absolutely no other explanation for how Bootsie got under your car other than that she was dead on that spot in the parking lot moments before your car and Munchie arrived, and you did indeed park over her. And we all know you're a little sensitive over your parking—"

"I am not! And I'm getting fed up with this parking topic. Let's say I parked over a body without damaging a single hair or picking up a trace on my car. That would be some pinpoint-decent parking right there. Barney, are you getting this logic?"

"I certainly can do something with that point," Barney assured her.

"Well," Mary Ellen continued as though she hadn't been interrupted, "And we thought it would be better together—"

"In a public fishbowl?"

"Together we can review, and all agree that that's what happened so when that goes into the official report—"

"It's already there," said CJ unhelpfully.

"And when the whole thing gets reported on WNEM TV and other local news outlets, you will be prepared and ok with any comments or questions people have about double parking over a freaking dead body, Poppy," Mary Ellen said in exasperation. "Even in this town, that's a very bad piece of parking."

Poppy was beyond fuming over this. Barney stepped in like the true advocate he was.

"Look. I would amend what you're saying here by adding that this is the logical, and so far, only, explanation for how the body got under the car, but I'm not prepared to concede the initial opening statement Mary Ellen made that there's no other explanation. There's always another explanation," said the lawyer who was adept at finding those.

"Sure," said CJ. "Maybe Santa, needing a quick spot to hide the body in his sleigh, scooted Bootsie under Poppy's van." When Barney glared at her, she finally looked away first.

"So," Barney continued, "the official report should read that the 'current working explanation' for Bootsie under the van—"

"You mean other than a house dropped on her, like in *The Wizard of Oz*," shouted CJ.

"The current working explanation," continued Barney, "is that the wide-bodied Odyssey with the bouncing dog inside it simply parked over Bootsie, so to speak. Is that a satisfactory draft of the language for the report? Please bear in mind that it's the truest," he pointed out.

"Ok," said Ed, despite CJ's look of disbelief. "I can live with that. Well, look at the time! I've gotta run. Noon Rotary."

"Poppy, are you ok with that language?" asked Barney.

Mary Ellen latched onto the new language thing. "I think that's a perfect description of the real situation here, Poppy. You did nothing wrong no matter how this shakes out. You didn't even get a parking violation."

"Because it's on private property," muttered CJ.

Poppy looked around at everyone, mollified. "I'm good!" she said. "Mary Ellen, let's finish this meeting at the Kaffee Haus. Barney, thanks for presenting the real situation here. Ed and CJ, I know you have to put something in the report about this unusual situation, and that seems fine. And Todd, always great—if occasionally strange—to see you!" she chirped.

"Meantime, I will be looking for the actual answer to this peculiar juxtaposition of a dead body and my van because we—and by we, I mean law enforcement—clearly haven't figured it out yet. Great to see everyone! Talk later!" And Poppy was gone.

Everyone glared at Barney. "I think that went well," he said without a trace of irony, and walked out.

16: The Feds

After the meeting at the library and a calming cappuccino at the Kaffee Haus, Poppy arrived home. Since no one greeted her at the door, she assumed that Barney had taken Babycakes for a walk. That should get the neighborhood drums beating. Poppy smiled to herself. Living in a small town had far more advantages than disadvantages. She'd get a text by dinnertime asking if that was Barney, again. Just then her phone signaled a text message from Chief Ed. As Poppy had seen him earlier that day, she was surprised.

PLEASE CALL THE OFFICE TO SCHEDULE
AN APPOINTMENT SOMETIME TOMORROW.
THANKS, ED

Intrigued, Poppy dialed the police office number. After a few minutes, Ed came on the line. "Poppy, thanks for responding so quickly. I'm finishing up the paperwork on the Mills' murder. As a witness at the scene, I'll need your version of the events. If you could come in tomorrow, we can clean up that paperwork."

Poppy agreed that the next morning would work. As she put down her phone, Babycakes and Barney arrived back from their walk. Babycakes, who was usually delighted to see Poppy, walked right by her and took a long drink of water. Barney walked over to the counter, picked up a treat, and gave it to Babycakes. Poppy scowled a little at being totally ignored by her dog. She knew Barney was a favorite, but he wasn't staying forever.

"Barney, I need to go to the police station tomorrow to go over the story of finding Terri Mills' body. Since CJ was there as well as two other officers, I don't feel like I need an attorney, but should you tag along just in case?"

"Honestly, Poppy, I think in this case I should be present. Your name is associated with two recent deaths. No one is suggesting you had any part in them as of now. I think it's good practice to have representation on any document."

"Thanks, Barney. On to my next dilemma. Mary Ellen's Mah Jongg tournament is this week. I really need to brush up. Have you practiced with the new card?"

"No, I haven't even seen it. Could I look at your copy? Maybe we could put out the tiles and recreate the hands. That is an excellent way to learn the card and visualize the possibilities."

Poppy jumped up, put her tiles on the table, and grabbed the current card. "Should we order takeout? Maybe just a pizza. I have salad makings here."

"Call Da Vinci's and get a large pizza, your choice of toppings. I'll run and get it while you make the salad." Barney put on his coat, scooped up Babycakes, and off they went.

●●●

The next morning, Poppy and Barney arrived at the police station. Ed greeted them by the door and told Buddy, who was at the desk, to hold all calls. If Ed was surprised to see Barney, he didn't mention it.

"Thanks for coming in, Poppy. Good to see you, Barney. I have the report here that I plan on sending in. It's just a narrative of the events at the Mills' house. If you could read it, and if you agree, then sign it at the bottom. Of course, Barney is welcome to read it as well. For clerical purposes, Barney, you will be listed as Poppy's attorney."

After the paperwork was signed, Poppy looked at Ed. "What do you think happened out there?"

"It's early yet, but my best guess is a domestic issue. I had very little contact with the family. Their house is isolated out there, with few neighbors. We'll continue our investigation. You do not need to be involved, Poppy. And please tell Mary Ellen—"

The desk phone rang. Ed looked annoyed as he picked it up. "What? Buddy, I asked you... Oh. I'll be right out. Thanks."

Ed stood up. "Thanks for coming in, Poppy and Barney. Let me show you out."

Barney and Poppy walked down the hallway behind Chief Ed. There were two people, a man and a woman in black suits, standing beside Buddy's desk.

"Chief Ed Swartz? I'm Agent Brent Weiss and this is Agent Amanda Weiss—no relation. Could we talk to you privately?"

Ed led the feds to his office and Barney and Poppy walked out of the police station.

"FBI in town?"

Poppy looked at Barney. "They were FBI? How do you know?"

"I'm pretty sure I'm correct. I wonder why they're here. They don't chase down local murderers. It must be for another situation. Interesting, for sure."

17: We've Been Badged

Poppy knew they'd been given the fast shuffle out of the police station, so something interesting must have been up.

Ed and CJ sat in the conference room with the Keurig and the two feds with the same last name: a woman and man team, sort of like Ed and CJ, except Amanda had the higher rank. Their curiosity was on overdrive, but they knew they couldn't record this conversation, so they turned off the device that ordinarily captured what happened in that room. From experience, they knew that the feds would decide what they got to know. Since they hadn't called them in—as they would have, for example, for even a local kidnapping or anything at all that smacked of terrorism—Ed and CJ were fine with it at this point.

Jurisdiction was a funny thing, and in the larger world, the jurisdiction of the city of Frankenmuth was very tiny compared to the entire United States. Anything could be up. Poppy had, oddly, had a jurisdiction conversation not long ago with one of her grandkids, who asked, "Nana, why do we see a sheriff's car there and a state police car over there, or a city car around town? How do they decide where to go?" It reminded her that people didn't automatically know these things.

Amanda spoke up after selecting a caramel macchiato flavored pod. "We won't keep you in suspense. And obviously none of this is to be shared with anyone at the moment, but we hope we can be helpful to one another. You assumed we are FBI agents, but we are from Homeland Security, working with Customs and Border Patrol, and we are here about the two suspicious deaths you've had. It's possible that these two deaths are related." Indeed, that was completely new to Ed and CJ. The two agents pulled out their badges for a quick showing. In the legal community, this was lightheartedly referred to as "being badged." It always seemed to confer a great deal of power on those with federal badges from any agency.

CJ was so surprised she couldn't help herself. "What even brought two deaths in a small town in Michigan to your attention? Do you guys really keep track of deaths everywhere in the US all the time? How do you do that? Good grief! These women were terrorists?"

Brent gave a tiny snort at the thought that they *would somehow have that kind of information spontaneously,* plus the immediate jump to terrorism, although that wasn't unreasonable. "No, we don't really have that information on our desk daily. The only thing worse than no information at times is way too much information. But in this case, those two names popped up because they are already on our radar, so to speak, and we have a local informant we have worked with periodically."

"Bootsie, the out-of-town Mah Jongg player, and a local housewife are on your radar and somehow connected?" CJ pressed.

Ed, usually impressed with how fast CJ was on the uptake, could see that she hadn't made the potential connection yet. "They could have a connection, CJ," he said. Looking at the officers across from him, he continued, "It's that they both might be connected to the import-export business, isn't it? At any rate, that will have to be clarified."

CJ agreed.

Amanda continued. "I know this is going to be very weird information for you. It even was for us. But we are looking into a wide circle of illegally imported ivory."

That certainly did stun both Ed and CJ. Ed was immediately thinking about the variety of imported goods in their little tourist town, and wondering what was going on. The big gift shops, heck, the little gift shops, too, the Christmas store—there were thousands of imported items for sale in town. There was no implication that any of the local businesses were anything but on the up and up. But it wasn't a bad town to make a few small things disappear among the huge number of other small things, although even that was just a thought at the moment. Between murder by caffeine, and Barney and the girls somehow connected to the feds, there was a lot to figure out.

"All of this is obviously confidential. This investigation is in the early stages. And you've got two murders on your hands, so we'd like to help out with that if things converge. Meantime, we have to head to a meeting with our informant who has been doing some traveling on our behalf."

Ed and CJ locked eyes briefly, wondering who that could be.

As soon as the federal undercover car left the parking lot, Ed said, "I'm not getting up from this computer until I make some kind of record of this visit."

18: That's Samantha, Not Karen

Poppy had saved tables at the Kaffee Haus so any local players for the tournament could chat and play and have a cup of coffee. She had set aside a couple of hours for this and sent out a general email to everyone signed up.

One woman walked in and immediately spotted tiles on Poppy's tables. She made her way over and said, "Hi, I'm Samantha from Grand Rapids, and I'm here for the tournament." Poppy smiled and invited her to have a seat to chat, and asked if she could buy her a cup of coffee.

Samantha sat down and said, "I don't see them roasting their own beans here. Really, I don't commonly drink coffee anywhere that I can't see the beans somewhere in that process."

Poppy said, "The beans here are roasted a few miles east of here and are genuinely great roasts."

Samantha sniffed and suddenly seemed to notice the Mah Jongg set on the table. "Surely that isn't a Walmart set, is it? It looks like it could be a Walmart set."

Poppy was now starting to feel a little defensive, especially after the intervention of her friends trying to get her to accept that she didn't notice a body in the parking lot. She rose to the occasion. "It's exactly a Walmart set. I'm not bringing a vintage set to a practice session. Anyway, it's more a symbol to draw players to the table."

Samantha was plenty experienced with putting someone in her place. "Those tiles will only scare people away who are looking forward to some serious play." She then pushed the tiles in Poppy's direction, but half a dozen fell on the floor.

After picking them up, Poppy invited the visitor to play a two-person game called Siamese in the Mah Jongg world.

"Sure, but let's play with my tiles," countered Samantha. She pushed the Walmart tiles in Poppy's direction.

"Did you say your name is Poppy?" asked Samantha.

Poppy nodded as she was putting away her tiles.

At that moment, two more players walked through the door. It was easy to tell because they indeed made their way toward the tiles, as any Mah Jongg player on the planet would have done.

Samantha loudly said, "Poppy! You're the one who killed Bootsie, right? I'm surprised you're out already."

Poppy was getting herself in a major huff when the other two women walked over and wondered if they could make up a table of four for a couple of games.

Ignoring the comment about Bootsie, Poppy introduced herself to the two other women who were, of course, also signed up for the tournament. The comment wasn't lost on them, though, as they looked furtively at one another.

Samantha pulled out an interesting set that looked like it could be old, but Poppy had never seen the material before in a set. It wasn't Bakelite. It wasn't modern plastic.

Although it looked like bamboo and bone, it was no bone Poppy had ever seen before.

But she didn't bother commenting on the tiles because she was still irritated by the whole Walmart conversation. Normally, she would have admired the flowers or the bamboo. They were nice. But they all set up walls fast and started to play.

Samantha was, however, determined to make annoying small talk. "So, have you two just arrived, and have you heard Bootsie is dead?"

The women were shocked. "Our Bootsie is dead? Where's Dennis? What happened?"

"Well, Poppy here apparently ran over her in the parking lot."

All eyes were on Poppy. "Excuse me! I didn't run over anyone. Get your facts straight before you accuse people. She was apparently murdered, and the weapon was an overdose of caffeine. I think that's now been released publicly. As to how that happened, it's murder by person or persons unknown. Not my car."

"Well, I guess it's public now, although that's the first I've heard," said Samantha. "I'll be coordinating the Grand Rapids contingent. Why do they think it was murder? Maybe she overdid it on coffee."

"Samantha, what was it you said you do when you're not doing ... this?" asked Poppy.

"I'm in the import–export business."

Poppy got a chill down her spine looking at this woman who looked to her like someone who could put a knife in you. Poppy certainly felt like a knife was buried in her own back. She thought more than one import–export businessperson seemed like a lot right about now. She needed to talk to Ed and see what was up with Samantha.

"I gotta run," said Poppy. "See you at the tournament! Bye, Karen," she chirped at Samantha and left her no time to react.

She picked up her inexpensive but perfectly useful set of tiles all clearly recognizable and walked out the door toward her van. So far, there wasn't anything fishy about the tournament, but there were odd crosscurrents in the air that she needed to think about.

NATIONAL
MAH JONGG
LEAGUE, INC.

19: THE REPLACEMENT

Mary Ellen had gotten an early morning telephone call from Jean, the new leader of the Grand Rapids Mah Jongg Club. Since Samantha had taken the title, this was a surprise, but not the business of the Frankenmuth players. The ladies decided to meet for lunch and then tour Fischer Hall. Mary Ellen waited outside the Zehnder's bakery entrance so she could catch Jean and take her to Z Chef's in the lower level of the restaurant. A snazzy, red convertible pulled into the parking lot, and a very tiny lady hopped out. Jean was no more than five feet tall and had bright purple hair. She rushed over to Mary Ellen.

"You must be Mary Ellen. I'm Jean Roy from Grand Rapids. Thank you so much for having us. It is terrible about Bootsie, but we will carry on with the tournament. What a lovely day. Traffic was not bad at all. I do love Frankenmuth. We used to come here every Christmas. Well, not Christmas, but around Christmas. We'd go to Bronner's and then eat a huge chicken dinner. Such good memories."

Mary Ellen tried not to look shell-shocked. This tiny dynamo couldn't be more different from Bootsie.

"Welcome, Jean. It's so nice of you to come. Let's go downstairs and grab some lunch. I have a schedule and tournament format for you." She opened the door for her guest.

"I'm glad to be here. I've been playing Mah Jongg for many years. In fact, I taught many of our members, including Bootsie. Our club is a mixture of beginner and intermediate players, except for Elsie and me. We are quite experienced. At one time there were four expert players, but Bootsie, well, you know, and another lady has moved. My, look at this bakery. Oh, I have such a sweet tooth. I must stop on our way out to get some goodies."

Jean had stopped talking, so Mary Ellen jumped in. "Yes, it an amazing bakery. Z Chef's Café is a buffet. The trays are here. I recommend the Michigan cherry–chicken salad from the first station. There are soups, sandwiches, and a hot selection further along."

"Salad sounds good. I am starving. I do need to get home for an evening meeting so we should probably get right down to business. I'm involved in many activities and always overschedule myself. You know the old saying, 'If you want something done, ask a busy person.' That seems to be me. I am on the arts council, school board—although my children are no longer in school, of course—my church board, and now I'm head of the Mah Jongg club."

"Ma'am, do you want the dressing on the salad or on the side?" The server who had been patiently waiting interrupted.

Mary Ellen looked at Jean. "We do have a lot to cover. Let's get our drinks and sit right over there," she said, pointing to a booth. She left Jean to decide on the dressing situation and walked over to get her bottle of water. She wistfully looked at the wine selection on her way. This lady was proving to be a challenge.

"I know you must get back so let's get right down to business. The schedule of events is simple. Who knows— if this tournament catches on, we might want to make it bigger eventually. But this week, we'll have a Meet and Greet on Friday at the Marv Herzog, followed by a dinner at Zehnder's, and a one-day tournament on Saturday. The Meet and Greet will be at the Marv Herzog Hotel and the tournament at Fischer Hall. The Marv Herzog Hotel has a list of all the restaurants in town and the Chamber of Commerce has a nice coupon and small gift bag for visitors that we will see everyone receives. How does that sound?" Mary Ellen had tried to get it all covered before Jean could speak.

"Well, I'll certainly look it over. That was a lot of information. Do you always talk so quickly? I will call you tonight with any changes or concerns I might have. This salad is delicious. I do love the idea of a private dining room for us; that way we can let our hair down and have fun. You do have a fun group, right? Our group is hilarious. Why, last year we had a small tournament that went on for ten hours because we couldn't stop laughing."

Mary Ellen felt alarmed, both at the idea that this was fast and complex information, and at the idea of playing for ten hours. "We do have a great group. But we do play right along."

"Of course, slow play is not tolerated. In fact, we fine people who play too slowly. I'll oversee watching for slow play and keeping the games moving."

Visions of Poppy explaining to Jean that thoughtful play was an excellent strategy, but with different words, popped into Mary Ellen's head.

"I doubt that will be necessary. Let's look at Fischer Hall and then you should probably start home."

20: CJ is Voluntold

Mary Ellen put her phone down on the counter as Todd walked into the kitchen. "Who was that?" Todd asked.

"It was Ed. He wants me to stop in this morning and go over my meeting with Bootsie. I'm sure I have nothing to add, but I'll stop on my way to town. After that, I'm going to run to Fischer Hall to see if everything is set up, then hopefully catch up with Poppy. She is running a rules clinic this morning."

"Why don't you ask Poppy and Barney if they want to come over for dinner. I'll put some steaks on the grill, and you can make a big salad. It might be the last time to relax before this mini tournament starts. Remember when you started? Just two groups of Mah Jongg players getting together for a few friendly games. Now it's a mini tournament with cocktails, dinner, and prizes."

Mary Ellen nodded and smiled. "It did blossom, didn't it? It will be fun. I think dinner is a great idea tonight. I'll be home by four o'clock to help get things ready. Love you."

Mary Ellen went into the garage and got into her sporty car. The top was up as the weather had turned chilly, but it was still a zippy ride into town.

The parking lot at the police station was empty, as was the lobby. Buddy, the officer on duty, came back to his desk as Mary Ellen started walking back to Ed's office. "Mrs. Freeman, he's on the phone. Please have a seat and he'll be right with you."

Mary Ellen and Poppy knew most of the police officers in town as they were a very visible force. They also knew them in conjunction with their private investigator business. Just then, Ed appeared and invited Mary Ellen into his office.

"Thanks for coming. I just want to go over your meeting with Bootsie Van der Veer. I have the statement you made in the parking lot after we found the body." He handed her a copy of the report. "Is there anything else you can add? Anything else you now remember?"

Mary Ellen looked at the short paragraph detailing her conversation with Bootsie.

"Honestly Ed, no. She was in and out in less than five minutes. I imagine her husband is torn up. I hear he is at the SpringHill."

Ed looked up at Mary Ellen. "How did you hear that?"

Mary Ellen didn't want to throw Kenzie under the bus. "I think Barney mentioned it."

Ed nodded. "Well, if that's all we have, I guess ..."

"Ed, the Mah Jongg group she played with will be coming into town. One of them surely knew Bootsie well. Maybe Poppy and I could do some detective work and ask around."

Ed looked at Mary Ellen and said, "Thanks, but I think I have a better idea."

He stood up and went to the door of his office. "CJ? Could you come here for a minute?"

CJ walked into Ed's office. "Yes, Chief."

"You know Mary Ellen is hosting a Mah Jongg tournament this week with Bootsie Van der Veer's group. I'd like you to do a little undercover work and ask some questions. We need to get a better idea of who she is."

CJ looked horrified. "What? My time might be better spent working on the Mills case. That's a bigger mystery, don't you think? I mean, we have a missing child. I feel that I could be very productive there."

"Honestly, CJ, that may turn out to be a domestic violence case. I've already notified other jurisdictions that we are looking for Jack Mills, with the car registered in his name. As it turns out, Marcia is staying with relatives. Her aunt just requested school records be sent to an elementary school in Rockford, Illinois. So, it looks like you are free to spend some time in Mah Jongg world."

Mary Ellen looked at CJ and smiled. "I'll email you the schedule of events. See you soon. By the way, dress is casual, but not jeans. And remember, it's only a two-day event—the Meet and Greet on Friday and the tournament itself on Saturday."

Having said that, Mary Ellen took her leave, still smiling.

NATIONAL
MAH JONGG
LEAGUE, INC.

21: Tap Tap

Poppy looked around the second floor of the library and figured everyone was there for the advance review of the rules. This was a pretty pro forma thing since Mah Jongg rules were set by the National Mah Jongg League, with a tweak or two each year or so.

She brought handouts that Mary Ellen had been good enough to prepare for her and passed out copies as players assembled. People were in high spirits and looking forward to the main event the next day.

A few people had brought sets for a little just-for-fun practice play.

"Here are the people who will be East," said Poppy, reading off the short list. The tournament, at a dozen tables, was small. "Every table is expected to complete five games an hour. Any table that doesn't complete five games an hour will be penalized and of course will be short a game for possible points. Not to mention missing the quick breaks."

A little snickering ensued. "She means you, Georgia!"

Georgia waved her hand in the air and laughed, adding, "No one better cost me points because you can't make up your mind!" Apparently, she was one of the faster players. It all proceeded in a friendly way.

Poppy emphasized one rule that always seemed obvious but still got discussed a lot. "Of course, anyone can still call a discard until the next player has put her tile on the slanted part of the rack or discarded it."

Poppy then went on to the next obvious thing until Georgia's voice rang out, "Or taps!"

This was a reference to a common table rule in parts of the country where someone picked a tile and quickly tapped it on the table, officially starting her turn. Those not familiar with the game would miss the significance. It cut players off from claiming a discard in a fast-moving game.

"Haha!" fake-laughed Poppy. "Tapping will just cost you your turn, Georgia, because players can call the discard until that tile is racked properly." Half the players gave a hushed, "Ohhh," knowing the reaction that was coming.

"I'm not having my time curtailed and possibly losing points in this tournament when a simple tap is all it takes to let everyone know it's my turn."

"Not according to the actual rules, and when we set this up everyone knew that we play by standard rules, not your idiosyncratic local rules," Poppy said with her usual diplomacy.

"Wait! Aren't you the one who ran over Bootsie and killed her? You're not in jail?"

"I didn't run over anyone," said a fed-up Poppy for what felt like the hundredth time.

At this point there was a lot of back-and-forth about tapping and running over Bootsie.

Barney walked in about then and said, "Sorry I'm late! I'm subbing for Maris, who was called out of town on a family emergency."

Since it was rare to have a man playing, things quickly quieted down. "What's going on?" said Barney. "Did I miss the whole rules review?"

At this, the whole room erupted with the tappers and the non-tappers getting heated. Non-tappers accused the tappers of not wanting to give other players a reasonable two seconds to decide on a discard, which was basically true. They viewed it as a legit strategy. Tappers couldn't see what the difference was and why a tap wouldn't be good enough.

Barney said, "Oh! Well, we'll just check the rules." Poppy rolled her eyes since the rules were obvious on this. But he was getting everyone to look at the back of her official card. "Oh look. Here it is. Right here. Number five: 'A tile may not be claimed for exposure or Mah Jongg after the player next in turn has picked and racked or discarded a tile.' Well, that's it then," said Barney. "It doesn't mention any other signifier like the Florida tap—or Grand Rapids tap. Haha."

Poppy glanced at Barney with an irritated expression on her face. "Yes. Just as I said. Those are the rules. Are we all set for tomorrow?"

People started visiting with one another in the usual good-natured way of Mah Jongg players.

Poppy, however, was beyond weary of people referring to her as the person who ran over Bootsie. She excused herself while others had fun with practice games. She was heading home to Babycakes, and she wanted to come up with a plan to run a parallel investigation of the two recent killings. This required talking to Mary Ellen to plan yet another strategy.

22: Samantha Strikes Again

Mary Ellen quickly drove down the hill to Fischer Hall. She had a few Mah Jongg sets with her to put on the tables. That would give her fewer things to do tomorrow. The hall looked great. There were two more tables than they really needed. Mary Ellen knew there were always people who couldn't come, or people who brought a friend.

She had just set up the last of four tables when the door opened. Mary Ellen looked up. She assumed a tourist had opened the door just to look around. This lady walked right in and stood in front of Mary Ellen.

"I'm Samantha and I am the new maven of Grand Rapids. You must be Mary Ellen. I have heard a lot about you. Have you ever run a tournament before? I have, and I'm happy to give you tips."

Mary Ellen looked a bit startled. "Hello, Samantha. I'm a bit confused. I met Jean for lunch early in the week. She indicated that she had taken over as the Grand Rapids coordinator. Have you spoken to her?"

"Jean? I doubt she has the expertise to handle this. Bootsie certainly didn't. Are these the tiles we will be playing with? I'll have my own tiles, of course. Did all of you do a giant Walmart order for tiles?"

"We expect all players to use the sets provided, Walmart or otherwise. It eliminates from any equation the possibility of a player showing up with a set, especially a vintage set, where the players can basically read the backs of some of the tiles. So, no need to bother yourself with any other tiles. I'm surprised you don't know that happens at many big tournaments." Samantha seethed, but she knew that was correct information.

"Jean said she would be here tomorrow. I think we'll wait until then to straighten this out."

"As I know we can agree," Mary Ellen said to Samantha, "it's not the tiles' quality, but the player quality that makes a good game. I will say I love a beautiful Mah Jongg set. As a matter of fact—"

"Excuse me. I am the best option to take Bootsie's place. I will have a little chat with Jean when she gets here."

"Samantha, are you here early? Are you staying at the Marv Herzog? It's a great place, isn't it?" Mary Ellen had never worked so hard to defuse a situation and try to not yell at this pushy, entitled woman.

"I live here now. I moved from Grand Rapids several months ago. I've played with your group at the library. I'm assuming you have a more elite group that plays somewhere else. I would of course be a great addition to your game."

Mary Ellen took a deep breath. "Everyone is welcome to play at the library. We have players of all levels. Jean indicated that the Grand Rapids group was similar. We are just looking to have fun, enjoy each other's company, and make some Mah Jongg memories."

"So, there is a grand prize? Money?"

"No, it's a friendly game with prizes, but not cash prizes. We'll have lunch here. May I give you a packet of the events?"

"I'll certainly need that. Give me all of the Grand Rapids packets. I can make sure they get them." Samantha was now tapping her foot.

Mary Ellen had had enough. "I will give you your packet. I assume you RSVP'd. We'll discuss with Jean tomorrow how we will arrange things going forward. Right now, I have an appointment. Thank you for stopping in."

Samantha took the paperwork and left, slamming the door behind her.

Mary Ellen pulled out her phone and called Poppy who answered on the first dog bark of her ring tone.

"Hello, my friend."

"I have news to share. Can you and Barney come to dinner tonight? Todd will grill some steaks and we'll have a salad."

"That sounds perfect. What time? Six o'clock?"

"Yes, perfect, and there will be wine. Plenty of wine. What a day! We'll talk later. See you at six."

Mary Ellen walked out the door and to her car. Samantha was going to be troublesome, but Jean probably knew how to handle her.

23: Dinner at Mary Ellen's

Barney was enjoying getting to know the players who were doing practice games at Wickson Library. Since Mike wasn't there, Barney had the status of being the only man in the room and, as in most situations, made the most of it, putting on some charm while playing fast games.

His watch dinged with a text from Poppy telling him dinner would be at Todd and Mary Ellen's house this evening at six. He shot a quick text back. "I'll meet you there since I'm still enjoying practice hands."

In fact, after sending that message, he watched a player named Freida expose tiles he knew were not in a combination that was on this year's card. "That hand is dead, Freida." She took a close glance and realized he was right; she'd made a mistake.

And it was Barney's turn next. He picked a tile and said, "I'll take that joker, Caroline."

She rolled her eyes at how very fast that had all gone downhill and handed him the joker.

Barney immediately declared Mah Jongg. What a fun game, he thought. It was nothing but relaxing after workdays filled with long hours and tension most of the time.

Barney was the last to arrive at the Freeman house, at five minutes past six. Everyone was outside on the patio since it was an unusually nice night for March, barely at the beginning of patio season in Michigan. He settled into a comfy outdoor chair while Mary Ellen poured him a glass of red wine.

Todd led with a question they were all wondering about. "What's going on in Kenya that required your presence, Barney? Or were you there as a tourist?"

"I'm doing a little legal work for the World Wildlife Fund," answered Barney, "specifically concerning the endangered African elephant herds and what the people directly on the ground with the elephants can use from the organization."

"Are they an American–based organization?" asked Poppy, wondering how far his license to practice law extended.

"No. They are based in Switzerland, but there are some American philanthropists who are interested in putting serious money into it. I'm not licensed to practice law in Kenya, but I am in Switzerland and the state of New York, so I said yes to exploring more for them."

Somehow, whenever there was a conversation with Barney Mead, there were always surprises. New York wasn't a surprise, but Switzerland was. When questioned, Barney just waived a dismissive hand and said, "Dad."

Poppy knew there was a lot of information that likely made sense that they weren't going to hear regarding the influence of Barney's dad. So, she branched out as Todd tossed steaks onto the grill.

"What do they mostly need, Barney?"

"What they need is, of course, funding and an international ban on killing elephants. The profit needs to disappear."

Todd, however, still had questions. "So why are you here in Frankenmuth?"

Barney, without giving away anything, simply said, "I can work from anywhere on this most of the time, and I admit I've formed an attachment to the town. I thought I'd even see if there might be a condo for sale that might suit me as a vacation spot."

Poppy, however, was considering that it might be more the limited charms of CJ than anything else that drew Barney back to town. But she certainly wasn't going to mention that. And at the moment, she was grateful that CJ and Chuckie had formed a bond.

The steak was cooked exactly right. Poppy was the first to break up the evening by mentioning that she needed to get home to Babycakes.

She said to Mary Ellen, "The Meet and Greet is tomorrow evening. Let's get together for coffee in the morning and see what last-second things need to be done."

"Sounds good," she replied. "And I'd like to talk to you about Dennis, Bootsie's husband, too." She set the time and said goodnight.

Poppy was struck by what she considered to be a hodgepodge of events and situations that might all be related—or not. Barney's presence in town indicated to her that there were connections she wasn't seeing yet.

24: Ann Smith Arrives

Ed had decided to tackle his email inbox when Buddy from the front desk buzzed him. "Chief, there's a Mrs. Smith here to see you. Should I send her back?"

"I'll be right out, thanks."

Ed walked out to the front. A lady with a brightly colored top, cropped pants, and sandals was standing by the front desk. "Hello, may I help you? I'm Chief Ed Swartz of the Frankenmuth Police Department."

"Chief, nice to meet you. I'm Ann Smith, from Grand Rapids, Bootsie Van der Veer's sister. I have some questions about her death. Could we go somewhere more private?"

"Of course, Mrs. Smith. Let's use my office. Buddy, please hold all calls."

Ed led the way. He offered Ann the chair. Before he could sit down, Ann started talking.

"Chief, we—my family and I—are devastated by Bootsie's death, and frankly appalled that we have not been able to plan a service. What is taking so long? What exactly is the problem? She was hit by a car? Was it hit and run? Dennis has been amazingly unhelpful, which surprises no one."

"Mrs. Smith, our investigation is ongoing. We have been waiting for a few agencies to get back to us with test results. At this point, we know Bootsie was not hit by a car. A car inadvertently parked over her body. We do know that Bootsie was in the area for business and her business partner and ex-husband confirmed that she had an appointment that Friday morning, but he didn't know with whom. She also met with Mary Ellen Freeman about a Mah Jongg tournament that was scheduled for the next week. Is there anything you can tell us that might help?"

Ann took a deep breath. "I know she was here on business with Dennis. They still own Van der Veer Electric. She also does work without him. He might not know where or with whom she was meeting. He really doesn't care as long as she makes money. Dennis is all about money. I do know they have large insurance policies on each other. I probably shouldn't have said that, but it's a fact. Is he responsible for her death?"

"At this point he is helping us with the investigation. Can you tell me anything that might be helpful?"

"Well, Bootsie is reserved—oh, was reserved," Ann pulled out a handkerchief and dabbed her eyes. "This is very hard. I go from angry to a crying mess every ten minutes. She was very smart. She loved Mah Jongg and was quite excellent. I don't play, but her group admired her strategy and knowledge of the game. She loved coffee. I wasn't surprised to hear she was near a coffee house. I don't know what else would help. I didn't talk to her on

Thursday night, so I don't know where she was going. I do know she expected to be home Saturday evening."

"I appreciate you coming, Mrs. Smith. Will you be stopping to see Mr. Van der Veer before you go home?"

"No. I have no intention of speaking to Dennis. I doubt if he would be thrilled to know I was here today. We are not friends."

"Do you think he could have killed your sister?"

"Honestly, no. He was a lousy husband and just not a very nice man, but a killer? No. However, there is that insurance policy, and I have an idea that business isn't that great. That's why they came over to this side of the state. Chief, I appreciate your time. I know I wasn't much help. We'd really like to make some plans. Please get us some answers."

Ed looked thoughtful. "We'll do everything we can, Mrs. Smith, to find out how Bootsie died."

As Ann stood up to leave, Ed asked, "By the way, if I might ask: Bootsie? It's an unusual name."

"She's named for my father's favorite aunt. My dad loved her laugh and her madcap adventures, so he named his daughter after her. I'll see myself out, and I'll be in touch."

25: Post-Dinner Chats

Mary Ellen and Todd cleaned up the kitchen and sat down with glasses of wine.

"That was a very pleasant evening. I got to know Barney last year, but I'm glad you got to chat with him. He's a very interesting man moving in a lot of different circles. His work in Africa sounded quite prestigious. The World Wildlife Fund does wonderful work. I saw a documentary on elephants not too long ago. They are magnificent."

Todd nodded. "He has a varied clientele: wealthy old ladies with crazy relatives, and the WWF. It seems odd that he's here."

"Well, he said he loves Frankenmuth and he wanted to come back. Right now, he can work from anywhere."

Todd took a sip of wine. "I thought he wanted to come for a festival. Plus, Poppy had no idea that he was going to be in town. I'll bet there's more to this story."

"Well, my guess is CJ has something to do with his arrival. She did pick him up from the airport. Although, I don't think they have seen much of each other since he's been here. I'll ask Poppy about it in the morning. I saw

Chief Ed this morning. He just wanted me to verify my conversation with Bootsie Van der Veer."

"Have they come to any conclusion about her death?" Todd looked concerned.

"No, her husband is still at the SpringHill, but her Mah Jongg group arrives tomorrow. Ed is hoping to get some information from them."

"Is he going to interrogate them all?"

"No, he's assigned CJ to mingle and sniff out anything that might be helpful. I did not get the impression that she was excited about this assignment." Mary Ellen was now grinning.

"Does CJ play Mah Jongg? Won't she stand out?" Todd had a little bit of a grin as well.

"No, but the Meet and Greet won't be all about Mah Jongg, so she'll be fine."

"I hope she doesn't bring her gun, ME."

"I hope she doesn't bring her dog," groaned Mary Ellen.

●●●

Poppy and Barney were greeted by a very put-out pup. Babycakes loved Barney and could not fathom where he had been all day. After several barks, some tall-girl dancing, and belly rubs, Babycakes settled down and chewed a treat while Poppy and Barney caught up.

"That was nice. Thanks for including me, Poppy. Todd's a great griller, but a little misguided over his team, the New York Giants." Barney stretched out his legs.

"It was fun. And I was fascinated to hear you were representing the World Wildlife Fund. How did you get involved in that?"

"I was recommended by a friend and had the time, knowledge, and interest in making sure elephants are protected. It's very rewarding."

"What is your focus? Habitat? I have done some reading about the plight of elephants in Africa."

"Most of my work on this trip was filling out forms and checking laws that relate to various incursions. After a few days there, I discovered that I could just as easily work from anywhere in the world." Barney got up. "Would you like a bottle of water? I still feel like I need to hydrate."

"No, thanks."

Barney returned with his water. "So, it looks like I have walked back into town after two murders have taken place. The one lady you drove over and the one you found. Has Ed gotten a handle on what happened?"

Poppy grimaced. "The one I drove over, Bootsie, is a visitor. You met her husband. They are divorced and own a business together. CJ will be at the Meet and Greet tomorrow to see if her Mah Jongg group has any information. The other murder, of Terri Mills, occurred just out of town where she lived. Her husband, Jack, is missing. He owns a business called Tchotchkes Galore. Ed has issued an alert on him. Ed's all over both of them." Poppy yawned. "I'm going to let Babycakes out and go to bed. See you in the morning."

As Poppy left the room, she noticed Barney getting out his laptop.

26: THE EARLY BIRDS

One of the reasons, thought Poppy, that Barney made such an easy houseguest was that they generally kept different hours. Poppy would sleep in a bit when she could. Barney never did and thus was more than happy to take Babycakes for her first morning walk. The little Boston terrier had quickly learned this routine and sat patiently outside Barney's room at around 5:00 a.m. Normally he appeared right at 6:00 a.m., ready to accompany her on her walk.

Today was no different—although Poppy didn't know what "no different" really was, nor would she want to disrupt it anyway. Poppy's house (which of course used to be Poppy and David's house when he was still alive) was in a relatively new housing area in town, and spacious. That was why she could have long-term company and not care. Plenty of room to stay out of each other's way.

Barney helped Babycakes get dressed in her reflective harness and secure lead, and off they went, stopping first on the front lawn for a peeing opportunity (for Babycakes). They trotted along companionably, Barney happy to comment on birds or squirrels that caught the dog's attention. And he was reasonably patient in letting her have that valuable sniffing time. As had become normal on this trip, they crossed Main Street and headed over to one of the older subdivisions in town, a relatively new route for Babycakes. Although Poppy didn't ask and Barney didn't volunteer, it wouldn't be long before one or perhaps several of Poppy's friends would mention precisely where Barney and Babycakes were seen and when.

The walk was about one pleasant mile long and ended up at a smaller split-level house, a style popular back in the seventies. Frankenmuth neighborhoods were well-tended through the decades, and only the architecture dated them to anyone driving through.

Barney and company walked up to the front door, which opened before he needed to knock. Chuckie flew out onto the front porch and snarled at Barney but allowed sniffing with Babycakes.

"You'd think that grumpy, hairy little guy would get used to me by now," Barney said, and CJ laughed and ushered them inside.

"Maybe in a few years," she kidded. "I've never seen a dog so set in his unfriendly ways, but he does like me. He's surprisingly decent company. Remind me to thank Poppy for putting him into my care for the time being."

This was the house CJ had grown up in and eventually inherited. She didn't hesitate to move back after both parents died.

CJ, in what many would call a surprising fit of domesticity, had coffee and scones waiting for breakfast.

Since both were efficient people, that was less than a fifteen–minute moment.

"Is that a new bathrobe?" Barney asked. And that was about the right amount of time for the two of them to spend on foreplay.

●●●

This was the part of the morning that truly puzzled Babycakes and Chuckie, because they got the bedroom door shut in their faces—something that was a strange experience to both. They laid patiently in the hall and waited.

The conclusion for the dogs was their mutual walk, part two for Babycakes. They walked around the block CJ lived on, giving Chuckie his needed morning exercise, and Babycakes had a chance to look for yet more birds and squirrels.

But eventually, CJ and Barney, who were both consumed with their work much of the time, talked shop.

"So, two murders, again?" teased Barney.

"And guess who's in town?" retorted CJ.

"These happened before I got here, and I am not representing either of your victims. I did meet the grieving widower. That's my big connection. He's quite a guy."

"He's still at the SpringHill and ready to go home." CJ sighed.

"What are your plans tonight? Would you like to go out to dinner?" asked Barney.

"I'm working tonight. I'm going to Mary Ellen's Meet and Greet at the Marv Herzog Hotel. I'm going to be an extra set of ears to see if I can learn anything about our victim."

"What about your other victim? Are they connected at all?" Barney looked over at CJ.

"I can't imagine how. They are both ongoing investigations, so I can't say much. The two murders seem to have nothing in common. One in town, the other in the country. Both women, but one a lighting designer and the other a housewife. Both were married, and both husbands are still on the suspect list. But I'm sure you know; an open mind is the best friend of an investigator."

CJ waved as she rounded the corner to her house. She and Chuckie changed into their police clothes (yes, Chuckie had an official looking bandana that said, "Canine Corps, Frankenmuth Police Force). Chuckie was so small, it was clearly a tongue-in-cheek thing. Regardless, they both made their way to work at the station.

Meantime, Barney and Babycakes kept walking back to Poppy's. As they crossed the street, Barney realized they were right in front of Mary Ellen's and Todd's house. It was a good chance to thank them for their hospitality.

Barney rang the bell and Todd immediately answered. "Barney ... and Babycakes, come on in. It's nice to see you again."

Babycakes ran into the house and jumped right up on Todd's recliner. She settled herself and looked very smug, as only a Boston terrier could.

Mary Ellen came out of the bedroom. "Babycakes! Did you come over for a chat? Did you bring Poppy with you?"

Barney came around the corner. "Good morning, Mary Ellen. I just wanted to thank you for a lovely evening last night. Are you getting ready for your Meet and Greet later? I hear CJ will be working it, too."

"Oh Barney, hello. Yes, and I have a million things to do. Thankfully, Todd has been helping so I'll be fine. Would you like a cup of coffee? I was just about to have one."

Todd followed Barney into the family room. He glared at Babycakes. "Did you find a place to sit?" Todd realized that didn't sound very nice, so he added, "Good girl."

Babycakes made a "humph" sound.

"I swear that dog doesn't like me."

Both Mary Ellen and Barney chuckled, but deep down, Mary Ellen was beginning to think Todd was correct. Perhaps if he sat with Babycakes on his chair … or maybe not.

Barney walked into the family room and stopped. On the table was a magnificent box with the lid open. He could see beautiful Mah Jongg tiles nestled in worn velvet. He couldn't help but pick one up. "Oh, Mary Ellen, these are gorgeous. Are they yours? How did you come by them? Did you know they are ivory?"

"They were left to me by a distant relative. I plan on bringing them to the tournament tomorrow. I know everyone will appreciate them. Odds are no one's seen an old ivory set."

Barney picked up Babycakes' leash and helped her out of the chair. "We need to get home. I have work to do, and I know you're both busy. Thanks again. I know my way out."

● ● ●

A while later, Babycakes flew through the door and headed straight to Poppy's bedroom, Poppy started her day, and Barney secluded himself for some intensive computer time.

Personal scenes of how Frankenmuth woke up played out everywhere in town. As for these residents—permanent and presumably temporary—they were all creatures of habit.

•••

CJ was already in her office, of course, completely focused on what steps she could take that day to get closer to a killer, or killers. She had four file boxes full of items brought over from Bootsie's office by a detective from Grand Rapids. One paper at a time went on her desk. Each then got categorized as potentially relevant or not relevant to Bootsie's death. Indeed, as Bootsie's sister mentioned, there was a substantial life insurance policy, based on their mutual business association, which would leave Dennis two million dollars in the event of her death from any cause. Of course, the exception to that would be if Dennis were proven to be the murderer. This policy took priority in the "relevant" pile. "Well, well, Chuckie," CJ said to the little dog. "We might have something important here."

Chuckie was happy to be CJ's official listener as he curled up in a corner of her office—now a regular visitor who was done making a break for it. The person in his life was right here, and when she wasn't, he had a comfortable crate, toys, water, treats, visitors, and a dog's life as life ought to be. For now, anyway.

Meantime, Poppy was listing all the Mah Jongg players who might have had a grudge against Bootsie from business dealings or even Mah Jongg, and cross checking to see if any of them also knew the Mills family, as well as background information on where Jack Mills might have voluntarily gone.

Mary Ellen was thinking through the details of their upcoming Mah Jongg tournament, and Todd was in the garage loading his car with items Mary Ellen might need.

Barney stayed busy. Whatever he was up to was anyone's guess. As always, he played his cards close.

27: Meet and Greet

Mary Ellen had everything set up in the lobby of the Marv Herzog Hotel. The Meet and Greet was to start at 5:00 p.m., but many of the Grand Rapids crowd were wandering around, checking out the view from the deck, and looking at brochures of activities in and around Frankenmuth. From conversations she overheard, many of the players were so impressed with all the things to do, they were thinking of trying to book an extra night. Grand Rapids and Frankenmuth both had tourist attractions, but each town had its own vibe.

Mary Ellen had set up a welcome table with the agenda for the two days, a list of players per table, and "My Name Is" tags. She hated these tags, but it would make it easier for players to find their tablemates. The bar would be serving wine and beer. Mary Ellen had brought several platters of cheese and crackers, as well as veggies and dip from the Cheese Haus mere steps away. They then had a six thirty reservation at Zehnder's for the family style chicken dinner. No need to fill up before that feast.

CJ and Poppy arrived at the same time. Mary Ellen had just a quick minute to give them the lay of the land before both groups started arriving.

Poppy looked at CJ and said, "Don't forget to take a name tag. You'll want to blend in."

"I take it you don't think I ought to use my uniform tag." For CJ that was a joke. But she was planning to blend in as well as listen in.

"Are you coming to the tournament tomorrow as well?" Poppy was putting on her tag. It had a little dog print in the corner.

"I'm not sure. I guess it depends on tonight."

Poppy looked at her player assignment and was happy she was playing with Mary C. Mary was a good player and would keep the table moving. The other two players, Joyce and Julia, were from Grand Rapids. Poppy went on a Joyce and Julia search while CJ walked over to a group standing at the bar.

"Well, this is very nice. Mary Ellen has done a good job."

"We haven't touched a tile, so let's wait and see how play goes. If this group is full of slow players, it's going to be a nightmare."

CJ moved on to a group sitting in the leather chairs that dotted the room. "So, what exactly happened to Bootsie? She got hit by a car, I heard. Is that correct? And Jean has taken her place as our leader? I assume this Mary Ellen will fill us in soon. Who is everyone playing with? I do not want to play with anyone slow!"

CJ was surprised that slow play was such an issue. She walked over and stood behind a couch where ladies were talking softly. She overheard one of them mention that

Samantha had come. CJ's gaze followed the direction they were looking. A tall woman had just walked in the door and was headed for the welcome desk. CJ walked over and stood behind Mary Ellen, who was seated at the desk.

"Excuse me. Are you in charge?"

Mary Ellen looked up. "Yes, Samantha. We met the other day. I don't remember seeing your name on the registration list."

Samantha sighed. "I thought you understood that I would be taking Bootsie's place."

"Jean has stepped into the position, Samantha. Do you know Jean? You two can straighten that out and let me know."

This was turning out to be quite a learning experience for CJ. With vying leaders and slow play, Mah Jongg seemed more than just a game. She looked over at an animated group that had formed on the deck. She stood against the rail to listen.

"Poor Bootsie. I heard she got hit by a car as she was crossing the road. What a horrible death."

"I don't think she got hit by a car. I think she fell and hit her head."

"I heard she choked on coffee and then fell down."

"Well, whatever, she got what she deserved."

"Joyce, stop. You know that isn't true. No one deserves to be murdered."

"Well, my house would be standing if the electrical was done the right way."

"And you have a new house, and insurance plus your lawsuit covered all the charges."

At that minute, Mary Ellen called the group together for a quick talk. Everyone went back into the lobby.

"Hello, I'm Mary Ellen Freeman, and this is my counterpart, Jean Roy. Grand Rapids ladies, thank you for coming. Frankenmuth, thank you for hosting our lunch tomorrow. You have all been given an agenda. You will find your morning tablemates listed on the back page. You might want to sit with them at dinner tonight and get to know each other. Jean and I are looking forward to a fun and exciting tournament. Grab your coats; dinner is just down the street. If you are driving, turn left out of the hotel. Zehnder's is the big white building on the right. Mahj on!"

CJ waved to Mary Ellen. As she was walking out, Poppy joined her. "Are you going for dinner?"

CJ shook her head. "No, I think I have some leads."

Poppy wanted to share in anything new going on. "Would you like some help? We are working together."

"Technically, we are not working together, but help would be appreciated. Thanks."

28: The Case Is on Fire

"Well, look at this," Poppy muttered to a bored Babycakes. After a couple long hours on the "interwebs" as only great grandmothers would say anymore, cross–checking Bootsie and her business interests to see if they converged with legal issues (criminal or civil) over on the west side of the state, Poppy hit the mother lode. She found Bootsie's business interests converged with legal issues. "Motive, Babycakes? I think so."

The local paper had a story from several years ago that brought together total destruction of a house that burned to the ground, and a lawsuit resulting from that. According to the press, the plaintiff was Joyce Wong.

The lawsuit against Bootsie's corporation, Van der Veer Electric, alleged quite a few things. Wong had documented a series of complaints regarding electrical work on the newly built and purchased home, for starters. The newspaper, presumably with the blessing of either Wong or her attorney, or both, had photos of the house showing issues for each of the times Wong complained to Van der Veer Electric.

Poppy moved her materials over to the police station and sat with CJ, showing her what she found. "Look here, CJ, at this photo of blackened walls around several electrical outlets—in the garage, in the kitchen, in the master bedroom. Plug in at your own peril, apparently."

"Whoa," CJ muttered, looked at the pictures. "And here's what everything looked like during construction. And the complaints were serious—sparks arcing where the computer multi-plug sat, numerous phone calls, and copies of letters—a persistent series of complaints, all with no resolution."

"Holy smokes!" exclaimed Poppy.

"Not a funny joke, really," said CJ.

"Oh, you're right. It's not. Look at the toaster picture." In addition to a blackened wall, the photo showed drywall falling apart as a result of fire damage.

"Here are some official photographs from the arson investigation, although no one's alleging arson in the lawsuit. They're alleging basically incompetence and lack of response."

"Doesn't matter," said CJ. "The arson team is going into an occupied dwelling that burns to the ground, where the owner barely got out alive, and doing an investigation. They must think in terms of whether anything that electrical company has touched is on the verge of spontaneous combustion and is putting lives at risk, including firefighters."

"The place isn't even recognizable after the fire," said Poppy. "And that's just the start. Joyce herself was sleeping when the place went up in smoke, and here are more pictures of damages to her directly, along with accompanying medical reports."

"Wait!" said CJ with genuine excitement in her voice. She had run a check on Joyce's car, a later-model Ford crossover. Up popped a few parking tickets from this town and that location.

"But here's the coup de grâce," exclaimed CJ. "Her vehicle had a parking ticket right here in town, in Zehnder's parking lot for illegal overnight parking, and guess when? Two days before Bootsie's body wound up under ... well, you know ... wound up dead."

"Please. I've heard it and heard it. Dead under my car. I'm fed up. So, someone who loathed her, no doubt blamed her for a series of bad scars due to fire, not to mention the total loss of her residence, happens to hit town to have some chicken over at Zehnder's while Bootsie herself is either here or on the way here," Poppy finished.

"That's the size of it," said CJ. They both walked across the hall to find Ed organizing yesterday's mail into the keep/toss/file color-coded piles. Both women knew he had to be a bit anxious to have waited a day to sort through yesterday's mail. The Tums were on his desk in plain sight.

Ed listened with intensity and said, "Finally, a break."

29: When a Cup Just Won't Do It

Ed grabbed his office phone when told Doc Adams was on the line. "What's up, Doc? I always wanted to say that," quipped Ed.

"Good one, Ed. First time I've ever heard that." They went way back together, and both laughed.

"The reason I'm calling, Ed, is I don't want you to go off on any wild goose chases as a result of the tox report showing a lethal amount of caffeine in Bootsie Van Der Veer's system."

"You're saying she didn't die of that?"

"No, she died of caffeine poisoning all right. But we, I think, can close in on the manner now which we couldn't before."

"I'm listening," said Ed, who was hopeful he'd learn something genuinely useful here. He wouldn't mind, actually, if it wasn't a murder, but more of a weird fall–type thing.

"Although various levels of toxicity can cause one's system, most particularly the heart, to go haywire— technical term there—leading to death, and for different people that can vary as to how much is lethal, I was thinking you would likely head off looking for someone spiking her daily coffee, for instance, like that ex-husband she shares a business with."

"You're not wrong," Ed responded.

"But I took another look at that amount and because this is such a rare type of death—only ninety-two documented cases worldwide ever, and certainly the first time I've run into it in my long career—I've been reading. A 25 percent blood saturation level is considered a lethal amount of caffeine, and your victim had a saturation level of 72 percent. Looking for a spiked cup of coffee likely won't do it.

"So, I pulled the autopsy photos to see what I might have missed or minimized. And I minimized an injection site on her left arm that I should have paused on more, but I'm doing that now. Indeed, people get so many vaccinations now and it was in exactly a spot where a vaccination might be, that I didn't quickly go there. And according to her medical records, she does keep up on boosters, including a flu shot not that long ago. But after looking at the tox report, I think that is significant and enough to put down 'means of death—homicide' on the death certificate, which hasn't been filed until now."

"Can you paint me a picture here? Is this like an injection of—well—espresso or something? Is caffeine ever a part of any medical treatment?"

"Yes, sort of, if you consider cosmetic treatment—notice I didn't say surgery, like with a certified plastic surgeon—medical treatment, this is one scenario that could have happened. In an attempt to reduce fatty upper arms, she sought treatment from someone who used as part of the process intradermal caffeine injections. Perhaps she'd had that sort of treatment before with some success. But the amount of caffeine in her blood is far in excess of what any medical professional would have used, and I find it hard to believe this is an accidental death."

Ed whistled under his breath and knocked back a few Tums.

"Can just anyone buy this much caffeine that could be used like that?"

"Oh, yeah. Right on Amazon. Where you end up going with all this," added the doctor, "I don't know. But it could take you in a new direction."

"Thanks," Ed said almost in a whisper, his mind already racing. "Thanks, Doc."

30: Caffeinated or Decaf?

Poppy, an enthusiastic coffee drinker, left Ed and CJ to the information she had uncovered about the electrical fire. CJ took over, diving into her computer, typing in the search bar, "How does caffeine cause death?"

After some cruising around, she settled on an easy-to-understand informational page from Cornell University's Cooperative Extension. Although any medical examiner, including Doc Adams, could tell exactly how too much caffeine can cause death, it was imagining how this could happen that took a little more digging.

CJ jotted down these basics, both on paper and as a copy-and-paste document.

"According to the folks at Cornell," noted CJ, "five to ten milligrams of caffeine is a lethal or potentially lethal dose." She continued the summary in her own words. "One-tenth of a teaspoon of caffeine powder has five thousand milligrams of caffeine. Twice that has the same caffeine as drinking seventy Red Bulls at once."

CJ muttered "whoa" to herself. Chuckie opened his eyes just enough to see if food was involved in CJ's exclamation.

As in, "whoa, what a great treat I have for you." He resumed his nap.

Caffeine powder was considered a dietary supplement and thus unregulated by the FDA. However, an Ohio teen who died as a result of too many Red Bulls at one sitting had the FDA reconsidering seeking jurisdiction over the use of caffeine powder and caffeine-containing food/drink products.

CJ pulled up Amazon and discovered that it was easy to order caffeine powder online.

Clearly, from what she was reading, it would be difficult to accidentally kill oneself with the normal sources of caffeine, namely something a local coffee shop served. But you could kill yourself or someone could kill you by putting caffeine powder into your food or drink.

This would result in a cardiac event caused by an arrythmia brought on by the caffeine. CJ created a written report to give to Ed.

• • •

Poppy stopped over at the Kaffee Haus to put this information on the back burner until later. Obviously, Bootsie didn't consume a bunch of caffeine powder and crawl under the car.

Pat and Sharon B. (one of three in town) were there, and Jonny, the excellent barista behind the bar tonight, started Poppy's drink as soon as he saw her.

With a real cup of cappuccino in front of her (she wasn't crazy about takeout cardboard cups), she greeted her friends. Pat commented, "So, I saw Barney and Babycakes out walking this morning."

Poppy rolled her eyes. "He's using my house as an office again, so Babycakes is delighted by the extra attention."

"Well," interjected Sharon, "I saw them too, over in Kay's neighborhood, and it wasn't just the two of them."

Poppy's eyebrow went up. "What are you talking about?"

"It was Babycakes, Barney, CJ, and Chuckie—I think that's what he's called—out for a stroll in a scene of absolute domestic bliss."

Pat nodded and added, "I was surprised how fine Babycakes is with that Chuckie, who never seems all that friendly."

They indeed had one over on Poppy in terms of interesting news. "Really? That actually is interesting. I wonder how soon Barney is going to mention his new dog-walking route."

The three women laughed and moved on to the subject of a trash run gone amuck. "We need to talk about this trash thing more in depth," said Poppy, having finished her coffee, "but I have to run. I think I might have some information to share with Mary Ellen and possibly Ed and CJ that can lead us, I hope, into a clearer picture of how Bootsie ended up under my car."

Pat and Sharon noticed that Poppy spit that out as if Bootsie intentionally had caused Poppy some inconvenience with her final resting place in life being under her minivan.

31: Ed Catches Up

Chief Ed was thrilled to finally have a solid lead in the Bootsie Van der Veer case. He put his accumulated mail back in his in-basket to focus on the information CJ and Poppy had just given him. Joyce Wong had a real axe to grind with Bootsie and Dennis. The parking tickets put her in town around the time of the murder. Ed reached for his phone to call the Grand Rapids police department. He didn't know the chief personally, but he did know one of the lead detectives there, Rod Masters.

After navigating the automated phone system for non-emergency calls, Ed reached Rod. "Rod, Ed Swartz from Frankenmuth. I need some background on a fire that happened there a few years ago, the Wong house. It may be tied to a murder here."

"Murder in Frankenmuth? Is that right? Wow. Let me think. A fire, Wong? Is that the house fire that involved Van der Veer Electric?" asked Rod.

"Yes, the house burned. All the people got out. It was a complete loss." Ed read from the info CJ and Poppy had brought him.

"Let me pull up the particulars. The house was burned, covered by insurance, rebuilt the same year. It included some injuries, none life threatening. Van der Veer paid a healthy fine, and I'm sure their insurance rates went through the roof. So, who died?"

Ed cleared his throat. "Bootsie Van der Veer. I can't say much more than that yet. I will tell you her husband, Dennis, is in town and was here when she was killed. He said they own the business together, although they are divorced. He might, however, have a substantial insurance policy on her life outstanding. The details of that are unclear at this point."

Rod chuckled. "Dennis Van der Veer. I do know Dennis. He is a hard worker. He has a quick temper. I think the company is struggling right now. Let me see what I can find out about him. I'll give you a call back tomorrow."

"Thanks, Rod. We'll talk then."

Ed shut the lights off in his office and walked out to the parking lot. Walking up the sidewalk was Dennis Van der Veer. "I'd like a few minutes, Chief. I really need to get home. I've been cooperative. I did not kill Bootsie."

Ed reached out to shake Dennis's hand. "Dennis, good to see you. And I thank you for your patience. Could you come into my office? I have a few things I want to talk to you about."

Dennis and Ed walked into the building. "Dennis, I just got off the phone with the Grand Rapids Police Department. It's standard procedure to check into the background of victims. I understand several years ago there was a house fire that you were responsible for? The Wong house?"

"Chief, how could that have anything to do with Bootsie's death? I did not kill her."

"But about the fire?"

"The company was deemed responsible. I had hired a few subcontractors who were not fully qualified and not at all competent. We paid the fine and insurance paid the damages. The Wongs were not seriously injured, and their house was rebuilt. Do you think that Wong woman had something to do with this? She's never forgiven me." Dennis was very agitated.

"Dennis, we are doing the best we can. I should have more information for you this week. I do appreciate your help. I know your sister–in–law, Ann Smith, is also anxious for a resolution."

Dennis leaned over the desk. "Ann? You've spoken to Ann? Oh, I bet she wants this resolved. She inherits Bootsie's part of the business. I imagine she had nothing good to say about me. Great. The Wong woman and Ann." Dennis was now for sure agitated. "What do I have to do to make you understand," he shouted. "I did not kill Bootsie!"

Ed stood up. "Mr. Van der Veer, I'll be in touch. Let me show you out."

Ed and Dennis walked out to the front door. Dennis pushed the door open and stalked down the sidewalk. Ed went back to his office. He quickly made some notes and put them in the Van der Veer folder. He would have to come back early tomorrow to organize his thoughts. On his way out, he grabbed his Tums.

32: East Side, West Side: The Tournament at Last

When people spoke of Mah Jongg tournaments, they could be talking about any number of tables and players, from a few for a one-day mini tournament to hundreds in big venues like Las Vegas that lasted for several days. This one focused on a few players in a Grand Rapids group and a few in a Frankenmuth group, to give them a little more of a twist than only playing those they normally saw every week. It was an east-side, west-side tournament. This was the first year for what was going to be an annual event, perhaps expanding as time went on, and excitement was high. The mayor, Mary Anne Ackerman, was opening the event to welcome the west-side players to town. She chose a trademark dirndl, which she somehow made fashionable, and included a circle of fresh flowers as a hairpiece. She was at that moment the most adorable mayor in the state, and beyond.

"Good morning, everyone!" she began. "And to our friends from the west side, welcome to Frankenmuth. While this is a small tournament, it begins a friendly rivalry, and we know how high the stakes become in rivalries that people look forward to each year. I'll be the impartial mayor today and just wish you the best—may the jokers be with you! And here's Mary Ellen and Jean—you know them both by now, the two tournament directors—to get things started. Have fun in our friendly town!"

With that, Mary Anne slid out the door, thinking that she could run around and greet tourists, getting her picture taken with whoever wanted one before the flowers became unwearable. She was a practical person.

Jean and Mary Ellen advanced to the mic, which, truth be told, was completely unnecessary in this small space with only a few tables. But it was a tournament and Mary Ellen decided it needed a mic for gravitas, plus she never knew when she might need to get louder. Jean seemed to have the ability to speak loudly on a dime. Having a mic in front of her gave Mary Ellen a sense of security about really being the one in charge.

Mary Ellen directed attention to the prize table, which sat next to a smaller display table. "You'll see some fun prizes, of course," she said, "as well as an unusual antique set that I inherited from my aunt recently. I thought you'd enjoy seeing it."

Someone shouted out, "I thought sets that old didn't have jokers?"

"You're right," Mary Ellen said. "But my aunt apparently found some old blank tiles that are a good match which serve as jokers if you're playing by National Mah Jongg League rules. Johni Levene managed to make a match. That set isn't a prize, though, just an interesting set I thought people might appreciate."

Mary Ellen clearly had more to say as Jean smoothly reached across and grabbed the mic, bringing it to her own face before Mary Ellen knew what happened. Indeed, Mary Ellen had thought it would be Samantha she had to look out for and was glad that it turned out to be Jean as co-director.

"Hello, Frankenmuth! I'm Jeanine, but you can call me Jean. We are delighted to be here. Let's not forget we have determined to use a table rule familiar to us west-siders and a time-saver for all to not bother having East break the wall! Thanks, Mary Ellen, for being so gracious about that!" And with that, she handed over the mic to a fuming Mary Ellen.

"Uh, well, let's move on to timing. You'll play six games, rotate tables with East and South moving, break for lunch, which is being catered by Tiffany's, with desserts supplied by the Frankenmuth players, and play six more games.

"You can see on the table right over there," she continued, waving her arm under Jean's nose and pointing to the only table without Mah Jongg tiles on it, "are prizes to be awarded to the top three places. You'll notice in this Year of the Dragon that the Covered Bridge Gift Shop has donated three spectacular pieces from the dragon section of the store. Any questions during play or disputes, just wave Jean and I over to decide. And as of ... NOW ... the clock is running. Play on!"

Sam (as Samantha liked to be called, at least by Barney now), Poppy, Barney, and Sharon B. were at table one, while Joyce, Jenny, and locals Pat and Mike were at table two. Each table had a set of tiles that were identical in style, in what was often known as the plain Amazon set that many people begin learning with. It prevented any confusion about what was a dragon and what was a flower, for example, if the two sets were well known and identical.

Play was immediately quiet and intense. Barney noticed what no one else did at his table: Sam's hand periodically brushing his right knee. He smiled at her when this happened, and she returned a sly wink. It didn't slow either of them up in gameplay, and the other players were focused on the game.

●●●

But there was one more person in the room who hadn't been mentioned, who most definitely noticed the "extra play" between Barney and Sam. That was CJ, who was monitoring the game, ostensibly as a "helper."

"What is this?" CJ wondered, watching the overt flirtation between Sam and Barney. He might not have started it, but he sure wasn't trying to end it, she noticed. And she was steamed. Their relationship, she thought, had been developing nicely.

Barney took occasional quick glances at CJ, and he recognized irritation when he saw it. But he was far from ready to remove Sam's hand from his knee—or what was it he felt now? A small advance north of his knee? He side-eyed a glance at CJ, thinking about how he looked forward to their morning "walks" with Babycakes, and now Chuckie. And still he tolerated what CJ perceived as a virtual assault. He knew she was hurt, angry, and armed, but would deal with it later.

CJ was so mad, she needed a breath of fresh air. She flung the door open with a bang, surprising Jean and Mary Ellen as well as most of the room.

Three things immediately happened when the door opened. The happy-go-lucky Munchie, tongue lolling, eyes darting around the room, and a mild look of uncharacteristic panic on his face raced in. Following that, a small white fur ball named Chuckie, of course, was right on Munchie's literal tail, snarling and biting. And third, Chief Ed was right behind Chuckie. He had volunteered to watch him for CJ, since he hadn't planned to leave his office. However, the sneaky Chuckie forced him to give chase.

The players were into game four, and play moved along.

It apparently never occurred to Munchie how much bigger he was than the ferocious Chuckie. "Chuckie! Chuckie!" cried CJ. "Come! Come here, Chuckie!" He glanced at her and wanted to run right over, but decided to bite Munchie first.

That bite really was the end of Munchie, who crashed into a table, sending Mah Jongg tiles flying everywhere. "Hey! Hey!" cried Sharon B., who didn't like Munchie to begin with. "That dog spilled water all over me!" Sharon stood up, shaking water from her shoulders to her knees. Munchie wasn't accustomed to being unpopular and wondered if Sharon was actually irritated with him. But no, he decided. No one was ever actually irritated with him.

While CJ could see that Chuckie was going to head her way and settle down, she didn't want to lose an opportunity in the chaos. "Whoa!" hollered Sam. "Who spilled orange juice all over me?" As she got up to run to the restroom and check the damage to her outfit, she slid on the ice cubes that CJ had spilt when she dumped juice and, although Sam didn't know what happened, Barney did. He had to help Sam off the floor.

Munchie was still on the loose and still in a panic since no one had offered him anything good yet. And Ed was using a leash like a lasso ineffectively focused on the innocent Munchie. Players were screaming and racing around the room. CJ sat down in a wet chair. "Here, Chuckie," she said gently, as he plopped on her lap, eyeballing the chaos in a pleased way.

But Munchie wasn't feeling the love yet, and Poppy was determined to calm him down. Just as it seemed she might pull that off—since she always had dog treats on her somewhere—the door opened again and two Tiffany's employees with the catered lunch rolled the cart in. The smell of sausage pizza—among other goodies—caught Munchie's attention far more than Poppy, and he made a charge at the cart.

Ed had called for backup because he just couldn't think of another similar situation and wasn't sure what else to do. There were a lot of women screaming, and two—well, now one—out-of-control dogs. "Get your dog out of here, CJ." She gladly picked up Chuckie and headed for her car.

"Yeah, thanks for bringing him, Ed."

When Munchie had hit the catering cart on wheels, he caused it to ram into the table with the dragons on it, every one of which were breakable, and they all crashed to the floor.

The panic was coming to an end, though, and Mary Ellen grabbed the mic and told everyone, "Lunch is on your own. Come back in three hours after Jean and I restore order."

Ed was irked that the local private eye had claimed the

privilege of restoring order in his town, especially now with three uniformed officers milling about wondering if there was anyone who needed arresting. In a remarkable diametric changing of places, Ed stuffed Munchie, who still had a piece of pizza dangling off the long hair on his nose, into his squad car to personally deliver him home.

This tournament would be talked about for years. Cameras had been open and filming, both Poppy and Mary Ellen had observed. Poppy whispered, "We'd better have a decent afternoon." She felt a giant smirk from the west side of the state.

Mary Ellen turned to the display table to make sure her antique set and its jokers was still in place, only to discover that it was gone. She was distraught. Someone must have shoved it quickly into a bag, leaving only two tiles almost hidden beneath the table. "Oh no! My set! My set I inherited is gone. Someone stole my set." On the verge of tears, Mary Ellen called for everyone's attention.

CJ came back in, surveyed the mess, and noticed Mary Ellen's distress.

"CJ, my beautiful antique set has been stolen."

CJ pulled out her phone and took all the information necessary for a formal police report.

"Mary Ellen, you can sign this tomorrow at the police station."

National Mah Jongg League, Inc.

33: Calm After the Storm

Mary Ellen had texted her friends Tammy and Bri to help with the cleanup and reorganization after the Munchie fiasco. Tammy and Bri had been unable to attend the tournament as they were teachers and had to work. Today, however, was a half day, so Mary Ellen's SOS resulted in an immediate response. No one on earth could reorganize a room like an elementary school teacher. In no time, the food was disposed of, the tables repositioned, and the tiles set up for afternoon play. After hugs and promises for a long catch-up over coffee and a few games of Mah Jongg, Mary Ellen waited for the tournament people to come back from lunch.

Jean and Mary Ellen had decided to play two rounds of four games and call it a day. The winners would be the top four players. Since everyone had benefited from a leisurely lunch, play went quickly. By 4:00 p.m., Mary Ellen and Jean were ready to announce the winners.

"Players! I want to thank you for coming and for your patience during our little snafu. Jean and I have tallied the scores. It appears that two winners are from Grand

Rapids and two from Frankenmuth. Jean, would you like to announce our fourth-place winner?"

"Thank you, Mary Ellen. I just want to say what a lovely—"

A voice from a back table yelled, "Jean, just announce the winner."

"Oh well, yes, the fourth-place winner is Samantha Campbell." There was a smattering of applause. Samantha stood up, shaking her head. "I believe I was distracted and didn't play my best." She winked at Barney.

Mary Ellen announced that Sharon B. had captured third place and Joyce Wong was second.

Jean said, "That leaves our first-place winner, who is Mike T. from Frankenmuth. Congratulations, Mike. You have won a gift certificate from the Covered Bridge Gift Shop. A round of applause for Mike."

Mary Ellen said, "Thank you all for coming. Please have a safe journey home. We would love to meet again for a rematch."

Poppy and Barney were packing up the tiles when Mary Ellen walked by and whispered to Poppy. "Meet me at Prost in half an hour."

By 5:45 p.m., Mary Ellen and Poppy were sitting at a table in Prost with a glass of wine. "Holy smokes, what a day! It was so good and so bad all at the same time. My antique set was stolen, and I had to fill out a police report. Karen and Rick List owe me big time. That horse that poses as a dog nearly ruined my tournament."

"In the end, other than your set, it really didn't matter, and no one will ever have put on such a memorable event," said Poppy. "By the way, did you see Barney flirting with Samantha? I know CJ saw it and I doubt if she is pleased."

Mary Ellen looked at her friend. "Poppy, why is Barney here in Frankenmuth? I get the feeling that this isn't just to visit CJ." Both women nodded hello to Father Bob as he passed their table, heading to one with friends further back.

Poppy commented, "Everyone loves that guy. He seems to be using retirement to get in some travel, and golf, but also to help in the diocese with funerals, weddings, and more."

Mary Ellen added, "And he's a one-man beautification committee." This was a comment on his gardening skills.

"Back to the main point—why the heck is Barney here in Frankenmuth, other than to see CJ?"

Just then a lady walked up to their table. "Mary Ellen? I thought that was you. We don't see you anymore on Craft Day at the library. Do you remember Terri? She was part of our group. She was murdered. I haven't heard anything more about her death. It's so unnerving."

"Margaret. Oh, my goodness. I haven't forgotten Craft Day; it's just I've been busy with so many other things. Retirement is exhausting. Margaret, this is my friend, Poppy Lutz. I did hear of Terri's death. I had forgotten that she used to come and craft. As I recall, she was very talented. She used to bring the library all kinds of materials to use for crafts and our maker's space."

"May I sit for a moment?"

"Of course."

Margaret sat and looked down. "Terri was a talented lady. I think things were changing in her life. I dropped her daughter off at home a few months ago and there was quite a security gate to get onto their property. I asked Terri about it, and she said that her husband's business equipment was very expensive, so they felt they needed extra security. She didn't invite me in as she had done in the past. The next time I saw her she said they were moving to Wisconsin. She said it was closer to family, but she didn't appear enthusiastic. I had heard that it was a random attack, which does not make me feel any better."

Mary Ellen reached over and took Margaret's hand. "If Chief Swartz thought there was any danger to the community, he would have issued a warning. I know he is on top of this situation."

"I didn't mean to disrupt your evening. I should go. Thanks for listening, and try and come for crafts. We miss you." With that, Margaret stood up and walked out the door.

Mary Ellen looked at her phone. "I'm going to text Todd and see if he wants to come down for dinner. Why don't you text Barney? Maybe he has some explanation for his interest in Samantha."

"Good idea. So, Terri's husband? What was his business equipment?"

"If I remember correctly, he made ornaments and decorative items for the house and yard. He also drove a truck, I thought. I remember Terri talking about him going to the Soo to pick up materials. You know, I think we need to pay Ed a visit to follow up on the theft of the antique tiles, sign the report, and also follow up with Terri's husband's business machinery. Let's do that tomorrow. Tonight, we celebrate that we lived through the Great Mah Jongg Mash!"

34: Ed Puts Things Together

Ed unlocked the door to the police station. He had gotten up early and grabbed a cup of to-go coffee from Biggby's so he could jump start his day. The door was locked at night even though there was an officer on duty. Buddy was surprised to see Ed at that unusual hour.

"Chief, I put all the new reports about the Van der Veer and Mills murders on your desk. I think there are a few still in your inbox."

"Thanks, Buddy. That's my mission for today. These murders need to be solved. I have a meeting with Mayor Ackerman this afternoon and I would like to have something concrete to share with her. Could you leave a note for CJ to find me as soon as she gets in? She was here late last night so she might be a little late this morning. And hold all nonessential calls, please."

"Sure thing, Chief."

Ed walked down to his office and sat for a minute, staring at the top of his desk. He pulled his famous colored folders off the organizer and proceeded to match reports to the appropriate murder. Most reports were obvious as to which murder they belonged to. There were the Van der Veer autopsy report, the Mills autopsy report, pictures of both crimes, toxicology reports, background checks, witness statements, and interrogations. Murders generated a lot of paperwork. Ed reread the information that CJ and Poppy had found last night, feeling like the Van der Veer murder had a good chance of being solved fairly quickly. It was just a matter of weeding out suspects. Someone was bound to make a wrong move. As he thought about the Mills case, though, Ed felt that the one motive they had was not as solid as he would like.

As Ed stood up to do some stretches, he spied the trifold board that was stuck behind his filing cabinet. Last year, Poppy and Mary Ellen had attached sticky notes to a Mah Jongg rug to display suspects and clues. They had transferred the notes to the trifold to look more professional, according to Mary Ellen. Ed smiled at the memory, then turned back to the task at hand. He turned his chair around again and grabbed the board. It had been helpful in keeping track of people and motives. The small police station didn't have room for a dedicated visual-aid space, so this worked.

Ed had just written the names of the victims on sticky notes and assigned each murder a third of the board when the office door opened, and CJ poked her head in. "Chief, I'm here. Do you need me?" She looked at the board and nearly laughed. "Seriously? The board?"

"Hey, thanks for coming in early. I need some help here. Let's go over reports and put notes under the correct victim."

"Why the trifold board? Why not two boards? I thought these murders were not connected." CJ looked puzzled.

"They're not. This was behind the filing cabinet, available and large enough to hold our information. I'll look at reports and tell you what to write. Your handwriting is better than mine."

"Ok. What's first?" CJ settled into the chair opposite Ed.

"Bootsie, under car. Put a small picture on the board as well. Terri Mills, stabbed in empty bedroom in house. Another picture."

CJ did the two notes for Bootsie and the cause of death for Terri. She picked up a small picture of the crime scene at the Mills house. She looked closer at the picture. She then sorted through the other crime scene pictures and filled Ed in about the part of the tournament before he arrived and had to call in backup.

"I spent yesterday looking at jokers, and cracks, and dots. It was quite a day. Oh, and before I forget, Mary Ellen will be in later to report a theft. Her antique Mah Jongg set has gone missing. She brought it to Fischer Hall and during the melee it disappeared."

"I'm still in disbelief that Chuckie made his way over there," said Ed.

CJ grinned. "Let's finish this. It got more chaotic after you left."

"Okay, so Mah Jongg connections but not enough to tie anything together. Bootsie's toxicology report shows caffeine poisoning. Terri's toxicology report is due today. Terri's autopsy shows death was caused by stabbing. Damn, this report is in the wrong folder. This is the Mills address, so … it's the Mills address but it's in Bootsie's folder. CJ, Bootsie was at the Mills'. It was on her GPS. I think these murders are connected. Start a column with commonalities in both cases."

35: Jack Demands Answers

Poppy and Mary Ellen arrived at the police station to find Buddy manning the front desk.

"Buddy, could you tell the chief that Poppy and I would like to see him?" asked Mary Ellen.

Buddy was a little afraid of Poppy and Mary Ellen after last year's arrest of a killer. Mary Ellen was wielding a shotgun and Poppy seemed to be able to take the guy down and handcuff him. "Well, his door is closed, so that means he doesn't want to be disturbed."

Poppy pulled Mary Ellen's arm and started walking. "Good. I'm sure it's just the people we want to see. Thanks, Buddy."

They were at the door before Buddy could call and announce them.

"Chief," Poppy said as she opened the door, "I think we have some information to share. Hope we're not interrupting."

They walked in and stopped in front of Ed's desk. Mary Ellen smiled. "Ed, you have a clue board. That is amazingly helpful."

Ed looked a bit annoyed, and CJ had a subtle smirk on her face. "What's up with you two?"

Mary Ellen said, "Yesterday, I realized I knew Terri Mills. She used to come to Craft Day at the library. She'd bring leftover materials from her husband's workshop to stock our craft cupboard. Last night, Poppy and I ran into another crafter who was surprised by the security system around their house. Terri said it was to protect her husband's business equipment. I thought he made decorative things as a hobby. Do you know what his business is?"

Ed cleared his throat. "Thank you, ladies, for coming in. I'll—" At that moment someone yelled from the front of the office, "I want to speak to the chief. NOW! I want to know what happened to my wife. Do you hear me? NOW!"

Ed and CJ ran out of the office, followed closely by Mary Ellen and Poppy.

"What is the meaning of this? Who are you? And why are you causing such a scene?"

"My name is Jack Mills and I've been told my wife is dead. What happened? I demand some answers."

"Mr. Mills, put your hands where I can see them. Do not move. Do you have any weapons on you, sir?" CJ quickly moved in to pat him down.

"Weapons? No. Or yes. I have a boxcutter in my pocket. What is happening? I am a victim. My wife has been killed."

"Sir, I'm going to read you your rights. Please listen carefully." Ed read Jack Mills his rights. CJ had taken the boxcutter and put it in an evidence bag. Ed handcuffed Jack and steered him into the interview room.

Poppy and Mary Ellen started toward the interview room door. Ed dismissed them. "Thank you for coming. CJ, please make sure the camera is working. Poppy and Mary Ellen, goodbye."

Ed went into the interview room to find Jack sitting with his head on the table. "Mr. Mills, you have the right to an attorney. Do you want to call one or should we provide one for you?"

"I don't need an attorney. I want to know what happened to my wife. She was supposed to meet me in Illinois. Her sister said she never came, and the police called and said she had been killed. What happened? Why am I in handcuffs?"

"Mr. Mills, we've been looking for you for several days. Where have you been?"

Jack sat up straight. "I've been getting our new house ready for Terri and Marcia; that's my daughter. I had all my equipment in my truck, so it had to be moved into the pole barn on the property. Terri was going to buy new furniture for the house. The kitchen stuff is unloaded. What happened?"

"Mr. Mills, your wife was stabbed to death at your old house. We've been looking for you for several days. No one knew where you were. You didn't answer your cell phone. Did your wife have any enemies?"

"Enemies? Terri, no. Who would stab her?"

"Mr. Mills, do you have any connection to Mah Jongg?"

Jack went white. He looked at Chief Ed. "I want an attorney."

"Interview ended until the person of interest has an attorney. Do you have someone to call?"

"No. But do I get a phone call? I'd like to call my daughter."

"CJ, I'm going to transport Mr. Mills to the Saginaw lock-up for the night. Can you cover?"

36: Closing a Door

Poppy and a couple of the Sharon Bs were in the Kaffee Haus somewhat ironically seeking out that caffeine buzz (caffeine poisoning had so far not put Poppy off her addictive drink, although she was thinking about precautions) when Sharon—whose chair looked out on Main Street—saw a state vehicle she'd never noticed before.

"Look at that," she said. All heads turned. The vehicle was stopped in typical traffic. "Michigan State Police Traffic Accident Reconstruction."

"Huh," said Poppy. "I wonder if someone had a car crash we haven't gotten wind of." They went back to their coffee and redundant conversations that everyone loved about the pluses and minuses of historical fiction. No one ever changed her mind.

●●●

Ed and CJ were watching out Ed's office window when the traffic accident reconstruction vehicle pulled in. They were, in fact, expecting the officer, Dave Bailey, with whom they had dealt before.

"Thanks for coming, Dave. I think you were faxed the reports so far about the body found under a car in a parking lot near here. We think we know what happened, but that won't help in court. We need an official report and because we do have a homicide on our hands, you stand a good chance of testifying eventually—we hope."

"No problem. This one is so different for me, I was anxious to be here. Normally I'm dealing with what happened when metal hit metal or otherwise crashed on the roads. Reading the reports, the medical examiner has fixed the cause of death of ... someone named Mrs. Bootsie? ... as caffeine poisoning, which, of course, I have absolutely nothing to add to. But the doc ruled out any injuries caused by being hit by a car, despite the body being found under a car. Is that about it?"

CJ and Ed both gave nods and yeps simultaneously. Ed added, "What we need is your opinion on how a body can logically wind up under a car—a Honda Odyssey, in this case—without apparently being touched by it. Let's go to the scene. Our vic's name is Bootsie Van der Veer."

●●●

"Well, look!" said Poppy. "Here's that state accident investigation vehicle again, followed by both Ed and CJ, and they are pulling into the Kaffee Haus parking lot. There better not be anyone under my van again." The other two looked down at their coffee and sideways at each other. Nothing would surprise them. In fact, they decided to stay right where they were while Poppy flew out the door to the parking lot.

Ed intercepted Poppy immediately. "Poppy! Just the person we were hoping to see here, or we would have needed to find you," Ed exclaimed with what Poppy thought sounded like forced joy. It was joy that didn't extend to Ed's face.

Introductions were made and Officer Bailey explained that he was there so that he could investigate and write an expert report on how Bootsie wound up under the Honda. "In fact, I hope that's your car right over there because I can get some measurements and take a look under it."

Poppy sighed and handed Dave the key fob. She was wondering for a split second if she needed to call Barney but hoped all this would work finally in her favor and put rumors to rest.

CJ, having apparently taken up mind reading, said, "You know the stories about this will outlive all of us in this town, Poppy, but this will give us what we will need in court someday, as well as being a more official exoneration of your driving. Well, not exactly that, but it will reassure people they aren't in danger of getting run over by you—well, that's not really going to happen either."

Ed cut her off before things deteriorated from there. Poppy was encouraged to stay by Dave in case he had any specific questions.

●●●

An hour later, they were all back in Ed's office. Dave explained what would happen. "I'll write all this up, including the firsthand interview I had with Poppy, explaining what was going on in her car with the big dog and the odd-steering van, as well as referencing the medical examiner's report. I'll put together all my measurements—glad to have had the exact same vehicle available—and my conclusion will be that you guys had it right.

"The effects of the caffeine poisoning dropped Mrs. Bootsie in her tracks in the parking lot. She was unnoticed by Poppy due to Poppy's having her vision and attention distracted by the large dog leaping back and forth in the front seat, and, thanks to the odd angle that Poppy normally parks at, that's how she ended up parking over a dead body. Neither the car itself nor the driver were responsible for whatever happened to the victim. Your analysis makes sense and will be supported by my report as well as any testimony necessary as things progress."

"Thanks," said Ed. "We will for sure need that. We don't want any defense distractions aimed at the car thing."

"This is the first accident investigation report I'll ever have written where there was no traffic accident."

Dave took off to his next stop while Poppy, CJ, and Ed felt everything possible had been done to shut that door.

"Coffee's on me," said Poppy, who was maybe the only person involved in this case who wasn't hesitating on her daily coffee routine.

CJ and Ed watched her leave with a bit of bemusement tempered with a drop of admiration.

37: Poppy Clears Her Name

Poppy was really fed up with people actually thinking she ran over and killed Bootsie. Frankenmuth had a long standing well-deserved reputation as a safe tourist town.

It was bad enough a while back—but at least personal and explainable—when an old lady was murdered in a tourist carriage. But who wanted a private eye who couldn't even see a pedestrian smack in front of her car?

Now, there was enough evidence available to let her off the hook, and it could all be made public. So, she set up a meeting with Ed, CJ, and Mary Ellen to discuss her public relations concerns as well as shift the focus to what really happened.

Poppy walked in with her own drink. Everyone else was willing to use the police department Keurig.

Ed was as anxious as Poppy to set the public record straight now that they had some facts and science to back it up. He just wanted to run through it before releasing it to the public.

"Good job, Poppy, digging into the use of powdered caffeine to kill Bootsie. Doc Adams diagnosed caffeine as the cause of death. Poppy, explain the scenario you and Mary Ellen have put together, please."

Poppy picked up the thread. "By now we've all read about the availability and lethal nature of an overdose of caffeine powder. There's no way Bootsie sat in the coffee shop and drank so much coffee she walked around and dropped dead. Indeed, she only had part of a cup of coffee there, according to those on shift, and seemed very jittery."

Mary Ellen chimed in. "Several people were in and out at Fischer Hall saying hello and talking about the upcoming tournament—and coffee was available. Bootsie was there for a while. But Fischer Hall is a pretty public space—tourists wander in and out if the door is open; they cut through from either direction as a sort of Main Street shortcut. Despite trying to figure out who was there, no one knows the whole picture of who was in and out."

Poppy confirmed that, adding, "I'd say very few of the people I saw in there were people I knew."

CJ took over. "It's also true that with Bootsie being from out of town, none of us knows where and how much of anything she consumed that morning. We all associated caffeine with coffee, but used as a murder weapon, it might have absolutely nothing to do with coffee. It could be put in plain water or anything edible or potable."

Ed said, "Here's a public statement I'd like to release to the press. At least here are the elements of it."

"Bootsie was poisoned with caffeine, exact method undetermined. But according to the medical examiner, enough to be lethal and cause cardiac arrest. She had been in the coffee house and left quickly because she wasn't feeling well. We also conclude that finding her body under the car of a local resident is entirely coincidental."

Ed continued, "Because the driver of that vehicle had a large dog momentarily blocking her vision as she was parking the car, she didn't realize that she had parked over Bootsie."

CJ interjected. "Can we add, please, that this local citizen did the most sensational parking of her life by parking over the body without the vehicle touching the murder victim."

Poppy glared at CJ but didn't see maliciousness in her demeanor.

"Well, uh, we probably don't need to add all that. But we can say that the medical examiner was clear that no car touched, hurt, or contributed to Bootsie's death in any way."

Mary Ellen, in a so-so-at-best attempt to comfort Poppy, added, "While it's true you'll be a joke around town for years, Poppy, this nonetheless clears your name."

Poppy had mixed feelings. While on the whole, this might not stop parking jokes, at least everyone would realize that she didn't kill Bootsie. While she was thinking this was a step in the right direction, CJ said, "If her detecting don't get you, her parking will! You could put that on your business cards. Lemons into lemonade." No one could help it. They all doubled over laughing.

Poppy sighed, forced a smile, took a sip of coffee, and said, "I'm not Bootsie, so I'm not taking this lying down."

Everyone else in the small station could hear laughter rolling through the building.

38: The Dinner

Poppy looked at Babycakes, who looked at her with that "you're not leaving me, are you?" expression. "No, I'm not, Babycakes. You've been alone a lot today and Mary Ellen and Todd love you like family. Get dressed!"

The little dog started dancing around and stood under her harness and leash, ready to put on her "clothes." She pottied outside and wouldn't need to again for a few hours. And she seemed to have some kind of secret language with Todd—Poppy thought it was mysteriously sweet.

Mary Ellen explained that Todd was the chief cook and would join them when dinner was ready. He was in the later stages that required attention. Babycakes sniffed the air and headed straight to the kitchen. Todd's voice carried through. "Well, hello, Babycakes. What a, er, great surprise." Mary Ellen, Barney, and Poppy settled into comfy chairs with glasses of wine, and everyone looked mellow.

Mary Ellen sashayed forth with the opening conversational gambit. "How're things going with CJ, Barney? What a pleasant surprise to see you two have become … closer."

Before Barney could evade directly responding—yet another of his verbal skills—Poppy added, "The whole town has noticed your very early morning walks with CJ, Chuckie, and Babycakes."

Barney sighed. "It's been great. I admire her professionalism and, well, everything else about her, and she has become a good friend."

"Then what's up with all that flirting at the tournament, for Pete's sake," said Poppy.

Barney's eyes inspected the ceiling. "How about you girls go back on the payroll so I can share information and, of course, use your help."

Both women let the "girls" thing go and signed on. But it was one of those things that was ok if they used it, less so if "the boys" did.

"What are you really doing here, Barney?"

"Well, seeing CJ truly is one thing I'm doing here, although she's currently a bit miffed at me, but she hasn't been written in yet on my real assignment. I hope that's going to be tomorrow—the morning walks are getting lonely. I'm an informant for US Customs and Border Protection."

"What! I thought informants are basically criminals who get paid for being on an inside track," said Mary Ellen.

"Well, yes, most of the time. But we are serving common interests and, since I'm not a fed, I can sometimes move in different circles.

My work for the World Wildlife Fund focuses on closing down the worldwide ivory trade, and the US wants to see the ivory trade end, too. Like any criminal enterprise, it brings organized crime with it, but whether it's a small or large organization—we aren't sure yet. But there's a local connection to Frankenmuth."

"So, it's a win/win to fight the ivory trade that we didn't know existed in the US," said Poppy.

"Exactly. I know there was obviously chaos at the tournament, and we have our eyes on even old ivory that's legally imported. Can I see your family Mah Jongg set, Mary Ellen? You were about to be read into all this soon anyway."

There seemed to be scuffling noises coming from the kitchen. Right at that moment, Babycakes ran like the wind, or her version of it, through the room, eyes bigger than normal, with a meatball in her mouth. Todd was on her heels making a concerted effort to put an end to the food pilfering while still trying to appear hospitable toward Poppy, who he was irked with for bringing an uninvited guest, and they kept going.

Poppy gave chase too because that's what she did. Mary Ellen and Barney resumed their wine sipping because, at this hour, that's what they did.

•••

Poppy returned with Babycakes and a half–eaten meatball in her hand. She handed the meatball to Todd and grimaced. "Sorry, that's a compliment to your cooking."

Mary Ellen stood up. "Todd, it looks like Babycakes approves of your meatball recipe. Poppy, let's keep Babycakes in here while Todd finishes up." She gave her husband "the look" as he turned to go back to the kitchen.

"So, Poppy, Barney just asked about my Mah Jongg set. I'm going to go grab it."

Poppy settled in her chair with Babycakes in her lap. "Mary Ellen, I thought it was stolen. You found it again?"

"It showed up on the front porch today. Let me get it and explain what happened."

Mary Ellen returned with the distinctive box and placed it on the trunk that served as a coffee table. She carefully opened the lid to reveal the neatly packed tiles.

Barney leaned over and picked one up. "These are beautiful. I'm so glad they were returned intact."

Mary Ellen put the two additional tiles on the table. "I pulled these tiles out to show the pattern. They must have gotten knocked on the floor during the commotion. As you can see, there is no space in the box for them. I don't think these are my antique tiles. I've already filed a police report today on the theft. When I go in to sign it, I'll amend it."

Barney looked thoughtful. "I'll be paying a call on Ed tomorrow myself. I've got some information to share with him. I feel like my work and his work have some similarities, or even connections."

39: CRIME SCENE INVESTIGATORS

Ed had been patiently waiting for the Michigan State Police Crime Scene Response Team to issue its report on Terri Mills's death. Unlike on TV, crime scenes took more than an hour to analyze and process data. Terri Mills's death had been violent, and although it seemed to be confined to a single space, investigators would examine all the surrounding structures and property.

Ed opened his computer to find Detective Gomez had sent his preliminary report. Ed read through the email and attachments carefully. It appeared that Terri had died from a stab wound to the neck consistent with a box–cutter–type weapon. The perpetrator was probably standing behind her and was left–handed. Ed started jotting down notes. There were fingerprints from at least nine different people who were in the house. Only Terri's, Poppy's, and Mary Ellen's were identified. That meant that no one in the house had fingerprints on file.

Ed read through the entire report before calling CJ into his office.

"CJ, I got the report from Crime Scene Investigators this morning. Terri Mills was stabbed, as we thought. Since Jack claims to have been gone, she was presumably alone in the house. There were no defensive wounds, so she didn't try and protect herself."

"Do we really believe Jack was gone?" asked CJ.

"According to a response from the Be On the Lookout we sent out, his truck went through the toll plaza on the Jane Addams highway in Chicago one hour before the earliest time of death estimate. That puts him at least four hours away. He lawyered up yesterday, so I'll have to find out who his attorney of record is. I'm pretty sure he'll be released. We booked him on suspicion of murder and clearly, he has a reasonable alibi."

Ed pulled out his board while CJ rolled her eyes. "CJ, it does help me organize my thoughts."

Buddy poked his head in. "Chief, Mrs. Lutz, Mrs. Freeman, and Mr. Mead are here. Should I ..."

Poppy walked into Ed's office. "Ed, Mary Ellen has an interesting story to tell you about her Mah Jongg set, and Barney has a—"

"Honestly, you two cannot just walk in here. We are right in the middle of several difficult cases. Ed can't take time out to listen to a Mah Jongg story." CJ had her hands on her hips.

Barney cleared his throat. "CJ, nice to see you. I think Ed will want to hear all the information that we have."

Ed stood up. "Have a seat, everyone. These murders are taking a toll on all of us. Mary Ellen, what can I do for you?"

"Thank you, Ed. I brought my antique Mah Jongg set to the tournament. As you know, during our lunch fiasco, it was stolen, and I filed a police report with CJ. Yesterday, it turned up on my front porch. However, I don't believe these are my original tiles. I took out two tiles to show their unique design. They must have fallen under a table. The returned set does not have room for those tiles and the design and color are slightly different."

"So, in addition to two murders, we have a Mah Jongg tile thief? Mary Ellen, I'm sorry your tiles were stolen, and glad you appropriately filed a theft complaint. Right now, we are focusing on murders. Thanks for coming in." Ed stood up.

"Ed, I know you are curious as to why I came along today," said Barney. "I have some information that may be connected to the murders and to Mary Ellen's Mah Jongg tile theft." Barney quickly filled Ed and CJ in on why he was really in Frankenmuth.

CJ looked incredulous. "Do you mean that you were assigned to come here? This is a job?" With that said, she left the office and slammed the door.

Barney looked surprised. "I didn't think she'd be that upset. I'm here to help."

Poppy and Mary Ellen nodded sympathetically.

"Let's talk about the case and focus on that," said Ed. "You and CJ can work on whatever it is you have going later."

40: REGROUPING

Barney, Mary Ellen, and Poppy decided to go to the Kaffee Haus to look at their options. Barney was convinced that the murders and ivory smuggling were somehow connected.

"I propose we look at the Grand Rapids players a little more closely," Barney said to what was now his local team again. "Bootsie was in town for a hot minute before she died. Her business was expanding here, so Frankenmuth wasn't an unusual stop. Her murder appears to be up close and personal, if not bloody. Ed and CJ are still looking at her husband, correct?"

Mary Ellen nodded. "That's a good idea, Barney. We could invite the group back for a rematch. I'm sure we could use Fischer Hall again. It could be—"

"Mary Ellen, no. We do not need another tournament—maybe ever. Let's focus on the people who might have a reason to kill Bootsie. Ed and CJ must not have any hard evidence to arrest her husband."

"Poppy, I think you're on the right track. Mary Ellen, you are the only one of us who met her. Did she talk about the players at all?"

"Barney, she said maybe a dozen words. The only things I learned about her were from other people from Grand Rapids. It seems she was an excellent player. That's about it."

The door to the Kaffee Haus jangled.

"Goodness, look who's here. My new favorite friends. May I join you?" Without waiting for an answer, Samantha pulled over a chair. "Barney, how lovely to see you. Mary Ellen and, I'm sorry, I seem to have forgotten your name, dear."

Barney looked a bit uncomfortable, but smiled, sat up straight, and introduced Poppy.

Samantha smiled. "Oh, yes." She turned her chair so she was sitting quite close to Barney.

Mary Ellen took a sip of her cappuccino. "Samantha, are you enjoying being in Frankenmuth? Is your business located here or do you have an office you have to travel to?"

"I work remotely. That was quite a tournament. My goodness. Mary Ellen, your Mah Jongg set is beautiful. You are lucky to have it. I'm always on the lookout for beautiful things."

Barney had gone to the counter to order Samantha a tea. He sat down and she leaned over and gave him a kiss on the cheek. "Thank you, sweet man."

Poppy tried not to laugh at Barney's discomfort. "Samantha, do you collect Mah Jongg sets? You weren't really impressed with our ordinary tiles."

"Oh. Poppy, I wish. You know who is quite the collector? Jean, Jean Roy. I'll bet she has twenty sets. She travels for business and pleasure and often sneaks in trips to antique shops, hoping to find a unique set. She loves coming here because of all the places to poke around."

Barney looked at Samantha. "She comes here often? What is her business?"

Samantha frowned. "Maybe pharmaceutical sales? Or travel consultant? I honestly don't remember. She's always on the go. So, Barney, I have a quick errand to run. Let's meet at Prost. Around six? Good to see you again." Samantha stood up and left.

Poppy looked at Barney and Mary Ellen. "Barney, you meet up with Samantha and get info from her. Mary Ellen, you contact Jean Roy and invite her for a game. I'm going to go get Babycakes and walk over to CJ's. We'll compare notes tonight."

41: Consolidating Efforts

Barney was getting ready to meet Samantha at Prost when he got a text from the agents Weiss: "Meet us at the police station in 15 minutes." Barney quickly texted Poppy and Mary Ellen about the meeting and directed both to meet him there.

Thirteen minutes later, Barney, Mary Ellen, and Poppy walked into the Frankenmuth Police Department. Buddy directed them to the conference room. Ed and the agents Weiss were already seated.

"Barney, this is a confidential, private meeting. Please have a seat. You two," Brent Weiss said, nodding to Barney's investigators, "will have to excuse us." He stood up to shake Barney's hand. Amanda Weiss held the door open so Mary Ellen and Poppy could leave. CJ took the opportunity to walk in.

Poppy and Mary Ellen went nowhere. Barney said, "Agents Weiss, may I introduce my investigators, Mary Ellen Freeman and Poppy Lutz. They have been very helpful with this assignment."

"Barney, this is an important federal investigation. We do not use random housewives as amateur detectives. Thanks, but I'm quite sure we don't need the extra assistance." Brent looked irritated.

Poppy stood up. "Sir, we are locals. People talk to us. We do not drive big, black SUVs that scream government. We do not scare people, and we see things that are out of place. We are also discreet and reliable. As I'm sure you are aware, there are two murders that seem to be connected to your federal case. Chief Ed has practically deputized us. We'll be staying."

Ed looked impressed, then concerned. "Agents, both Poppy and Mary Ellen have been helpful with this local case. If you think the cases are connected, they should be included. But just to be clear, they are not deputies."

Barney cleared his throat. "As a matter of fact, I am meeting someone who may have information at 6:00 p.m. Mary Ellen, did you get ahold of Jean Roy?"

"Barney, who are these people you're referring to, and how are they connected to ivory smuggling?" Amanda said.

"They are Mah Jongg players from the Grand Rapids area."

Amanda looked up from her iPad. "According to your last report, Bootsie Van der Veer was at the Mills' address before her death. The Mills woman was found dead the next day. Is there an ivory connection?"

"There is a good chance that Jack Mills is involved in ivory smuggling," Barney confirmed.

"Jack Mills has been cleared of murder charges. And I agree there's a strong possibility he is involved with ivory," agreed Ed.

Brent stood up again. "I think that Barney and Ed are correct. I don't think Jack Mills is the mastermind in this area. He might be a middleman. I think our best move right now is to see if Jack can lead us to the next level. Ed, can you arrange for Jack to be followed? I'll work on telephone communication. Poppy and Mary Ellen, do you have anything to add?"

Mary Ellen looked at Poppy. "I'm going to contact Jean Roy. She is the head of the Mah Jongg group from Grand Rapids and was a friend of Bootsie's. She seems to spend a lot of time here. She may have some insight on players from her group."

Amanda looked at Mary Ellen. "What's her name? J–E–A–N R–O–Y? I'll do a quick check on her to see what I can find."

The Weisses stood up. "Let's reconvene tomorrow at 11:00 a.m."

As they left the meeting, Poppy thought she heard CJ tell Ed that she would be out of the office for a while.

42: DIGGING FOR DIRT

Barney walked into the back door of Prost. At six o'clock, the bar was full, but a table by the front window was available. Barney asked the hostess if he could sit there. He also explained he was expecting a guest. The hostess said, "No problem," and brought him a small leather-bound binder with wine, beer, drinks, and food options. It was a very comprehensive menu. Barney quickly chose a Michigan-based craft beer.

The beer arrived quickly, and as Barney was taking his first sip, he happened to look out the front window. CJ, Chuckie, and Poppy were walking right in front of Prost. Barney raised his glass as a salute. Neither of the women nor the dog acknowledged him. Chuckie was excused as he probably couldn't see in the window. But Barney recognized a deliberate snub when he saw it.

At that moment, Samantha approached Prost from the other direction. Barney hoped Chuckie didn't take a chunk out of her leg. Fortunately, she opened the door and made her way to Barney's table unscathed. Instead of sitting across from Barney, Samantha pulled the chair next to Barney, closer to him, and sat down.

"Hello, good looking. I've been anxious to get together since the tournament. We had such a great connection, don't you think?" Samantha smiled and snapped her fingers at the servers standing by the bar.

Barney looked pained at the entire performance. "It's good to see you as well. Here's a menu."

"I know what I want. I'll have a bottle of Prosecco, the best you have." She turned her back on the server and leaned into Barney's space. At that moment, Poppy, CJ, and Chuckie walked in front of the window again.

Barney was feeling uncomfortable, but he knew he wanted information from Samantha.

"Samantha, this is a good chance to get to know each other better. Tell me, what brought you to Frankenmuth? Your job?"

"Oh Barney, it's such a great town. There is so much to do here, and I found the perfect house. Tell me about you. What kind of law do you practice? Family? Criminal? And why are you here? I Googled you and you don't have local offices. I thought Poppy said you were here to visit her. Are you friends? More?"

Barney took a long sip of beer. "I am a longtime friend of Poppy's. I was also great friends with her deceased husband, David. I don't have offices here, but much of my work can be done remotely."

Samantha looked at him quizzically. "I always visit my lawyer in person. You don't have clients who like to talk to you in person? Or are you working on a case that is perhaps different than your usual business? I thought Poppy had said you were just back from Africa."

Barney realized that Samantha was also looking for information. This was going to be tough. Her name had not raised any red flags, she didn't seem to live extravagantly, and while she knew Bootsie, she didn't have a connection to Terri Mills.

"I did travel to Africa for a safari. It has been a dream of mine for years. I love travel, and seeing the people and animals of Africa was amazing. Have you ever been?"

Samantha started to speak. "I haven't had the opportunity. Is that Poppy? And the female police officer?" She stood up and waved. Both ladies waved back and kept walking. "Anyway, I don't travel much, yet. I, too, have a bucket list, and travel is on it."

"Samantha, I thought you would travel more in the import–export business. That's an interesting business. What exactly do you do?"

Samantha looked at Barney with big eyes. "Import–export? Who told you that? I am a representative for various cosmetic companies. I encourage stores to carry the brands in my catalog. I do travel, but only in the upper Midwest."

Barney finished his beer and looked at his phone. "Samantha, this has been lovely, but I have a few calls to make. Thanks for meeting me. We must get together again."

Samantha stood up and took out her wallet. As she did, Barney could see inside her purse. Samantha carried a gun. Interesting. Not criminal, but notable.

She gave Barney a hug and a kiss. She snapped her fingers again at the server. Barney said, "Samantha, our drinks are taken care of. See you soon."

They each walked out different doors: Barney to the back parking lot, and Samantha out the front door right in front of Poppy, CJ, and Chuckie

Chuckie started growling and barking. Samantha looked more annoyed than anything.

"Are you girls stalking me or Barney? I saw you walking in front of the window. I assume one of you has an interest in one of us."

Poppy laughed and tugged on Chuckie's leash. "Chuckie, cut it out. Good to see you, Samantha. We are trying to socialize Chuckie. He is a rescue and CJ would like to be able to take him out in public. The benches on this side let us walk him, then sit as people walk by. It's going to take some time, I'm afraid."

"Well, I hope you have some luck. It appears he has a long way to go." Samantha stood on the corner waiting for the light to change.

"Do you mind if we walk with you? We're parked behind the Cheese Haus. We can do the same process over there. Walk, sit, walk."

Samantha shrugged. "Sure. Just keep that beast under control. He's still growling."

CJ smiled. "At least he hasn't bitten you. We are making great progress."

They crossed the street and Samantha walked past them. "Good luck with the dog."

CJ and Poppy followed a short distance behind her. Their real mission was to find out what kind of car Samantha drove. CJ had been unable to find a car registered to Samantha Campbell. This seemed odd.

Samantha got into a white panel van. CJ took out her phone to take a picture of the license plate. As she zoomed in, she swore. "Damn. That van is covered in mud." Spring in Michigan brought out farmers and tractors preparing the ground for planting. She looked at Poppy. "I'm going to call Buddy over on Cass Street in his personal vehicle. He can follow her to see where she goes."

"What else do we know about her? Does she have any connection to the Mills? Can you drop me off at home? Will Buddy call you with Samantha's destination?"

"Sure—let's go, Chuckie."

CJ was annoyed that Poppy seemed to think she could find out information about a suspect that the police couldn't. She sometimes wondered at Ed and Barney's insistence that these two amateurs were not just allowed but encouraged to participate in an ongoing investigation.

43: Letting Go

Poppy made sure that she had no meetings or obligations the next afternoon so that she could take care of personal errands. She got home around four o'clock, not feeling especially good about the day. But at least there was no reason to have a discussion with anyone until she felt like it.

However, she hadn't figured on Barney—the "extra" person in the house. He came into the study, where Poppy was putting away some paperwork, and he had two glasses and a bottle of wine with him.

"Too soon to talk?" he said. She should have known that somehow Barney would notice that there was a different car in her garage.

He didn't wait for an answer but poured both glasses. "You know, Poppy, with absolute certainty, that you didn't run over anyone."

"But that car," she sighed. "That car, despite what CJ thought, was like a talisman. It's like I could accomplish anything, find any dog, get to any spot, throw anything into it, and it was a wall of defense and protection. Now all I can think is there was a dead woman under it, and I didn't know it. How were you so fast to spot the change anyway?"

"I always glance through the garage window to see if you're home yet. And there's this gray, square car. How far did you have to go to find a Range Rover? Don't those things get like six miles per gallon?"

"I didn't ask," she responded, "but it's halfway to Detroit to find a dealer."

"From what I've heard, you'll be seeing that dealer a lot."

"It's dog friendly," she said, ignoring the Range Rover review. "And it doesn't look anything like the old Odyssey."

"Let's back up a few years, Poppy." Her eyes teared up. "Both of us might benefit from a long conversation about when David died."

She pushed her empty glass toward him so he could refill it. "We might be here a while."

He did, and they were.

44: Mary Ellen Chats with Jean

Mary Ellen got home after the meeting at the police station. Her assignment was to call Jean, the new maven of Grand Rapids. Jean had talked a lot each time they had met, but not about herself. Mary Ellen poured herself a glass of wine and put in a call to Jean.

The phone rang twice before Jean answered. "Hello? Mary Ellen? How are you? I was just about to call you. I'm going to be in Frankenmuth later in the week. I'd like to stop by and bring you a little thank you gift. Your group was so welcoming."

"Jean, I'd love to see you. A gift is not necessary. That's a long way to go for just a thank you. I do remember you saying you came this way fairly often. Do you travel for business?"

"Oh, Mary Ellen, I'm semiretired. I do have a little home-decorating business. I love to find various old and unusual items for my clients. I have several shops and auction houses where I hunt for goodies. The owners know what I might be interested in, so they will put things aside for me."

She's a collector, Mary Ellen thought. "I think I heard that you had quite a collection of Mah Jongg sets. Where do you find them?"

"I do have several sets. I rarely play with them because some are fragile. It's amazing how many sets end up in antique warehouses. Mah Jongg has really become popular recently. Many sets have been discovered in boxes that have other items, sort of a hodgepodge. I love to buy a box to discover a Mah Jongg set. Your set is very beautiful. I understand that it was passed down through your family. That makes it special."

Mary Ellen took a sip of wine. She decided not to share any information about her missing, now returned set, and the inconsistencies. "How interesting. Do you collect for a specific client, or just things you think you might use? Your Mustang is a hard car to haul things in."

"Actually, I have several self–storage units around the state. I have a system for keeping track of my inventory. I take pictures of all my acquisitions, so I know where everything is. You know those units are so handy. You can rent for a few months or long term. So, back to my trip to Frankenmuth. Should I call you or just drop in? I have your address."

Mary Ellen looked concerned. "You have my address? Did I give it to you? I think you should call just to make sure I'm home. Jean, it's been great talking to you. I guess I'll see you soon."

"Great! Bye, Mary Ellen."

Mary Ellen grabbed her notebook and jotted down some interesting things that Jean had told her. The storage units and her frequent trips around the state might be important. Hopefully the meeting tomorrow morning would help narrow down the suspects.

45: Ed Talks to Dennis

Ed arrived early to have some quiet time at his well-organized desk. He was thinking back to not all that long ago, when two other murdered bodies littered the city limits of Frankenmuth. He was sorely tempted at this point to propose to the city council that the police force be beefed up by one detective, an additional canine officer, and some additional technology in the office.

On the other hand, he didn't want to ask for these things. It would be like giving up on the long-time nature of the town as a very safe place to be. This wasn't yet a trend, he decided, and the temporary addition of assistance from Poppy and Mary Ellen—he almost hated to admit—was enough to make him feel they could put a quick end to this murder streak.

Then he asked Buddy to find Dennis and tell him the chief needed to see him.

Thirty minutes later, Dennis came in, touchy as ever.

"Good morning. Did you call me in here to tell me I can go home now? I do have a business to run, and running it from a hotel isn't working for me."

"Well, Dennis, you might stand a chance of going home sooner if you'd tell us everything that could be seen as relevant."

"I have absolutely nothing relevant to Bootsie's murder to tell you. We haven't been especially close since the divorce."

Ed was a good deal more irritable than Dennis that morning. He plopped a document between them that was labeled "Long-Time Security, Inc."

"What's that?" Dennis said.

"That's the two-million-dollar life insurance policy that I know you've already applied for payment on."

Dennis was so taken aback that they seriously thought it might be him who killed Bootsie that his voice took on a more worried tone. "Well, yes. After the divorce, Bootsie and I—as business partners—purchased identical insurance policies on our lives where we named each other as the beneficiaries to protect our business interests should something happen to one another. That's all."

"If something happens to one another? Like what?" queried Ed.

"Like getting hit by a car," said Dennis.

"Is that a joke, Dennis? Do you see me laughing?"

"I'm sorry. Indeed, that was a poor choice for an example—although as we both know, Bootsie was not hit by a car."

"Well, you were quick on the trigger, Dennis, applying so fast for this policy payout. I've gone through this whole document, and murder by anyone—not just you—makes this unenforceable. Yet, you were trying to get them to pay it out anyway. Why is that?"

"Because I need the money!"

"You are not in the clear," explained the irritated chief. "But, and this should be a mood lifter, if I haven't arrested you in seventy-two hours, you can at least go back to Grand Rapids. Even if it turns out someone else killed your ex-wife, you could have other fraud charges pending. I'm happy to let Grand Rapids enforce those laws.

"You can leave. But you're being watched."

Dennis slammed out the door, feeling worse than when he walked in. Ed on the other hand felt a little better, but he couldn't quite identify why. He still couldn't arrest anyone, which was, of course, the goal.

Out of nowhere, Chuckie appeared and sat on his foot.

46: Filling In the Feds

Early the next morning, Mary Ellen pulled into Poppy's driveway and tooted the horn. Poppy and Barney had been waiting by the door and came right out. Babycakes stood in the window looking very put out that her favorite humans were leaving.

"For goodness sake, Mary Ellen. Why is the top down?"

Ignoring that, Mary Ellen said, "Good morning, Poppy. I have your favorite cappuccino right here. Hop in. Barney, I didn't get you anything, but we can stop by the Kaffee Haus before we go to the police station."

"Ah, thanks Mary Ellen. I'm going to take my car. I have some errands to run after our meeting." Barney got into his car, laughing at Poppy's displeasure.

Mary Ellen parked next to the big, black Suburban that screamed official government vehicle. "Are they supposed to be incognito?"

Poppy laughed. "There are quite a few government officials who live in Frankenmuth, so I assume that a government car would not be totally out of place."

Barney, Poppy, and Mary Ellen met at the door and walked in together. Buddy directed them to the conference room. Ed and the agents Weiss were discussing policing styles, local versus federal. Ed had just finished explaining the relationships that were necessary for successful policing in a small city. He looked up as the trio walked in.

"Buddy, tell CJ that we are ready to begin. And pull up a chair so you can start us off with your information. Let's go around the table and share any updates. CJ, welcome. Maybe you can tell us what you and Poppy discovered yesterday."

CJ gave her report to Ed and copies to the agents. "After not being able to find a car registered to Samantha, Poppy and I made sure we ran into her. We walked with her to find out what kind of vehicle she was driving. She pulled out of the parking lot in a white panel van. It was covered in mud so I could not see a license plate. Buddy trailed her south on Gera Road."

Buddy stood up. "There was a lane closure in front of Bronner's. I did not make the cut, so I lost her. May I leave?"

Ed nodded. "Yes, and thank you for your effort. Mary Ellen?"

"I spoke with Jean Roy. She has an interior design business and multiple storage units in different locations. She will be in town soon as she wants to get together. I think Poppy and I can do more looking at her."

Barney looked over at the agents Weiss. "I have a proposal. I would like to suggest to Samantha that I might have connections in the ivory trade. She knows I've been to Africa. I think if she is on our radar, this might be a way to either clear her or connect the dots."

The agents Weiss quietly spoke to each other. Agent Brent Weiss said, "As an asset we do not want to put you in danger, but that could work. We will stay in close proximity to you at all times. You will tell us of meetings, times, and places."

While Barney looked pleased, Poppy and Mary Ellen looked worried.

Ed then wrapped the meeting up. "I am keeping an eye on Dennis Van der Veer. He had financial motivation to murder his wife. If, as we go forward, we decide the two murders are not connected, I have a good suspect for Bootsie. The department has put a twenty-four-hour tail on Jack Mills. He may not be a murderer, but he is involved in smuggling. I'd like everyone to keep in contact with my office. We'll set up another meeting as needed."

Poppy and Mary Ellen stood up to leave. They were headed to the Kaffee Haus to discuss their next steps. Barney sat with the feds to sketch out his plan.

47: What Defines a Waste of Time?

Poppy and Mary Ellen were enjoying a cup of coffee at the Kaffee Haus and thinking over where the heck they all were on the latest set of homicides in Frankenmuth—a thought neither of them imagined they would ever have.

Mary Ellen said, "Well, there are the suspects you know and then there are the suspects you don't know. We have a few. What we don't know is if any of them actually killed anyone."

Poppy agreed. "I'm obsessed over the killing technique with Bootsie," she said, glancing down at her very own cup of caffeine. "Where are you most likely to buy concentrated caffeine? Why would anyone want it since such a small amount of it is lethal? Is it the new Kevorkian suicide of choice? Did Bootsie kill herself as a last act and crawl under my particular car?"

"Oh, good grief, Poppy," said her friend. "This isn't all about you. You didn't even know each other."

"But my car was high profile," Poppy pointed out.

"I have news for you. Your new car is even higher profile. Whatever possessed you to run down by Detroit and get a

Range Rover? Did you lease it? I read everyone leases them because they don't hold up well beyond two years."

"That's crazy," said Poppy defensively. "That Acorn TV character, Vera, has driven the same one for at least a decade."

"That means nothing. Each episode, the car is used for five minutes max and then put in a garage until another show is filmed."

"Well, never mind all that," snapped Poppy. "Let's say all my cars are irrelevant. I've been asking myself where one gets this concentrated caffeine. They ought to sell it like ammo, behind a locked case. What else would you use it for? Yet, despite the FDA's best efforts, I find that you can get what amounts to caffeine bullets right from Amazon. So why don't I investigate the background of our list of suspects and see what we can see regarding their Amazon purchases."

"Not a bad thought," said Mary Ellen. "Will Amazon just turn those over to you? I'm thinking not really."

"If Ed secures a search warrant looking for that particular purchase on Amazon, Amazon has a way of complying with it. Surely only one person on our suspect list would be making such a buy. And because Amazon—I've looked— has lots of these supplements available, it's kind of the obvious place to make a purchase."

"Ok. You spend some time on that and hopefully get information quickly, and I'm going to check out some local gift shops that sell imported items."

•••

After a discussion with Ed and CJ, they decided this was a worthwhile lead regardless of what it did and didn't find, and Ed arranged to secure search warrants for the Amazon accounts of Dennis, Ann, Jack, Samantha, and Jean.

Poppy hustled back home with those. "The way this works," she explained to a snoring Babycakes, "is I fill out their forms, entering the information from each individual suspect, submit it, and we wait."

This was somewhat tedious but still doable in a day. That certainly didn't guarantee Amazon's normal lightning–fast service for this sort of thing, though, so a little patience was in order. *If they take too long,* thought Poppy, *they could bug who are for now the local feds to try their own order.* They had a way of making everything look urgent.

"Come on, Babycakes," she summoned. "Let's go take a romp near the river." Babycakes was standing under her leash that hung in the hallway, her face pointing intently, before Poppy could finish the thought.

Essentially a day and a half had been spent coming up with the plan, Ed securing the search warrants, and Poppy sending in all the paperwork. It felt like a lot of work with no guarantees, but Poppy figured no matter what they did or didn't find out, it would be useful and not a waste of time. Or so she hoped.

48: Sleuthing with Mary Ellen and Poppy

Poppy pulled into Mary Ellen's driveway and blasted the Range Rover horn. Mary Ellen came right out. After she had settled in the car and finished looking around, she said, "Poppy, I really like this car. It's quite nice and certainly has all the bells and whistles. Do you think the dogs are going to destroy it?"

"I bought seat protectors for the back so I think there will be little damage. The only dog who rides in the front is Babycakes, and the leather cleans up beautifully. Did you get ahold of Jean again?"

Mary Ellen pulled a piece of paper out of her purse. "Yes, and she told me the names of her favorite antique places in our area. I think we may be able to find out where her storage units are by showing interest in a big item that would need to be delivered and casually asking if they ever deliver to storage units."

"That sounds like a plan. Where is the first store? Bay City?"

Mary Ellen looked at her paper. "Millington. Millington's Treasures. It looks promising. Jean mentioned it first and said she is always very lucky there. That would give her access to storage close to Frankenmuth or right in Frankenmuth."

Poppy turned the car south on Gera Road. There were many ways to get to Millington using side roads but, in the spring, chances were good the roads would be muddy, and Poppy was unwilling to turn her new Range Rover into a mud mobile.

At the light at Birch Run Road, Poppy waited to turn left. Mary Ellen looked out her window. "Poppy, turn right. I think I just saw Samantha in that van. She's headed down toward Meijer and the outlet stores."

"Well, I'm in the wrong lane. We'll go straight and turn around. You keep your eye on that van."

Poppy pulled through the light, made a quick turn, and ended up waiting for the light to turn left. "Can you still see the van?"

Mary Ellen sighed. "No, but let's look at Meijer. She might have pulled in there. Go behind the store. I imagine there is a vendor door."

"Vendor door? Trafficking in smuggled ivory? Are you okay?"

"Just verifying what she told us. She could be telling us the truth. If she's not there, we can swing over to the outlets and do a quick drive through. If we find nothing, we head to Millington. Two birds, one stone, Poppy."

Poppy went behind the large Meijer building. There in plain sight was the white panel van and Samantha unloading several boxes. Samantha looked up, recognized the girls, and looked annoyed. She walked over and knocked on Poppy's window. The window slid silently down.

"Are you following me? I don't understand what your sudden interest in me is."

Mary Ellen leaned over. "Hi, Samantha. We were just going to pick up a few things at the store. We use this way to avoid stop signs and pedestrians. How are you?"

Samantha snorted. "I have work to do. Goodbye." She walked back to her van and started opening boxes with her box cutter.

•••

Poppy slowly made her way around the building. "Umm, so that doesn't put her in the clear, but it leaves room for other people to be considered. Like Jean Roy. Let's go to Millington and see what we find out there. Mary Ellen, you might want to call Barney and give him a heads–up. He's going to connect with Samantha today to see if she takes the bait."

Mary Ellen used Poppy's phone to call Barney so everyone was on speaker. Poppy said, "Samantha was indeed delivering to Meijer, and it might have been cosmetics as she claimed. By the way, she also has a box cutter. We're going to look at some places Jean Roy shops. Have you talked to Ed this morning, or Brent and Amanda?"

"I did speak with Ed. He interviewed Dennis again. Dennis has a clear motive for killing Bootsie but no connection to ivory or Terri Mills that they can find. He has a short fuse, but that's not a crime. You keep doing your research. I'm meeting Samantha for dinner."

"Great, see you later. Be safe."

•••

Millington's Treasures was right on Main Street. The girls walked in and were impressed and amazed at the number of booths. They spent some time browsing and marking item numbers down. After about a half an hour they approached the counter. A gentleman with a name tag on that read "Bud" greeted them.

"What can I do to help you?"

Poppy smiled. "Bud? We have several items we are interested in. We are interior designers and have a number of projects going. Is there a chance that you offer delivery?"

"We do offer delivery, for an additional price, of course. What pieces may I help you with?"

Mary Ellen had her paper in her hand. "The items on this sheet. First, of course, is there a discount for bulk purchases? Our friend, Jean Roy, recommended you. We would love the same discount you give her, and delivery to the same storage facility."

Bud looked at the paper and wrote down the item numbers. He then looked in a spiral notebook. "Jean gets a 10 percent discount and half-price delivery to her unit. You say you are in the same facility, the one on Gera Road, right off 46?"

Poppy smiled. "Yes, Bud. That's excellent. Mary Ellen, do you have our company credit card?"

Mary Ellen started digging in her purse. "Oh no, I left it at the office. Bud, we'll be back this afternoon. Thank you so much."

The girls left quickly. As they got into the car, they high-fived each other. "Let's try the store in Bay City. Ed may be able to get into the storage units with a warrant."

49: Who's Zooming Who?

Prost was again Samantha's choice to meet Barney for a light dinner and, more critically, drinks. She was convinced this lawyer wasn't just in town to visit friends, but she had no idea why she felt that way or why it would concern her at all. Just a vague feeling. Something about the guy just always seemed awfully serious. But it could be just her, she thought. Sort of her experience with lawyers.

Barney had arrived first because that was just who he was. If anyone got a choice of tables, he wanted it to be him. Prost had a good reputation, so he was happy with Samantha's choice. She seemed interested in him—perhaps—and he was most definitely interested in knowing more about her. He picked a table in the outdoor area that was attractively fenced off from the public sidewalk and warmed by a pretty spectacular fire pit. He also picked his own seat so that he could see who came and went while he was there. He always wanted to have a concept of who he was sharing the room with.

He stood when she arrived, and he was impressed with her appearance. Both men and women took a glance at Samantha as she greeted Barney with a peck on the cheek—a close gesture but not over the top.

He wasn't shadowed by the girls tonight. CJ had cleared up the question of the car. Indeed, Samantha did have a van she drove to town and more about that was being investigated at the police station. He'd leave that to them.

"So, Samantha, now that you're living in Frankenmuth, do you miss the Grand Rapids big city shopping?

"I love checking out the little shops for gifts; you know, just recreational shopping. For the kind of shopping I like to do, it compares well. Some people have changed over to doing almost all their shopping online, but it will—to me anyway—be a sad day when I open an Amazon account.

"I noticed in the local paper that there's a regular open Mah Jongg game at the public library on Thursdays, and I joined a few months ago. That's how I ended up on Mary Ellen's list of possibilities for trying out a small tournament here in a tourist town. Grand Rapids is by far the bigger city, but it isn't quite as, let's say, cozy as Frankenmuth. The small group I belonged to in Grand Rapids also thought it would be fun."

They each ordered a charcuterie board, something the restaurant was noted for.

"Well, you know what? I like it here. But I'm having a hard time putting you here in town at all, Barney."

"First," he responded, "I live in a community pretty close to here and not on par with the big city feel of your hometown, and I practice law in a few states, including all over Michigan, for starters. I have friends here and enjoy it."

They both looked at each other and sipped their drinks. Barney knew the conversational score at the moment was 1–0 and he was ahead, although it was subtle.

"I do a little business in some of the local shops here and all over the state, selling a few things wholesale to the retail shops. Not a huge business here, but this town does have a lot of shops," she finished, slipping off a shoe under the table and touching Barney's leg with her bare foot. She considered him a pretty cool customer since he didn't blink at the come-on.

Each clearly had their own agenda, and both concluded that, even if they hadn't, they didn't want to spend too much time with the other. Barney loved dogs. Samantha had little use for them. Samantha fashioned herself a big-city snob while Barney knew Samantha would be lost in, say, London, Paris, Madrid, or Istanbul.

Barney picked up the bill, and they parted ways on the sidewalk with another peck on the cheek no warmer than their initial one. But, thought Barney, the evening wasn't wasted, and he headed on foot back to Poppy's abode and the genuine adoration Babycakes greeted him with.

50: Poppy and Mary Ellen Take Charge

Poppy and Mary Ellen had just gotten into the car after checking out the Antique Emporium in Bay City. "It's the same story as Millington," Mary Ellen said. "Yes, Jean buys items and yes, they are delivered to a storage unit. We can let Ed know, and he can search it. Poppy, I need a cappuccino. Let's go to the Excited Goat. They have great coffee and delicious brownies. I think we need to take charge. We know the suspects and the victims better than anyone on this case. I think if we put our heads together, we can get this mystery solved."

The two friends and investigators ordered their drinks and sweets. Poppy looked over at Mary Ellen. "Do you have paper and pencil? I didn't bring my backpack, just my wallet."

Mary Ellen started digging through her purse. She pulled out Kleenex, an empty checkbook, a wallet, two lipsticks, and an emery board. Finally, she triumphantly held two pens in the air. She looked down at the table and took her brownie and Poppy's cookie out of the bags. "Go up to the counter and buy three more bags."

Poppy looked at her quizzically. "Why?"

"Let's make some clue bags. We don't have the big clue board, but we can write down what we know on the bags. It should work. One bag for each suspect. We know the victims and I think we know who is eliminated."

Poppy thought that was a brilliant idea and brought back the bags. The girls got to work. "Let's talk as we write," Poppy said.

Mary Ellen printed a name on each bag: Samantha, Jean, Dennis, Jack, and Ann. "I'm adding Ann Smith, Bootsie's sister. Inheriting half of the business is a strong motive. I think we'll eliminate her very quickly."

Poppy turned the bag with Samantha's name toward her. "Okay, let's get Samantha's info down. She is from Grand Rapids, moved here, has to have some kind of storage for her work, has been pretty interested in Barney." She looked at Mary Ellen. "He's a great guy, but she really zeroed in on him. She's left-handed; I noticed that when we played Mah Jongg. She's very assertive. She has no Amazon account, and no registered car. That's a good start."

Mary Ellen pulled Dennis's bag in front of her. "Dennis is the husband of Bootsie, from Grand Rapids, expanding business here, has a temper, business in trouble, benefits from Bootsie's death. No connection to Mills. I think we may be able to put him in the not-likely pile, agreed?"

"Yes, I agree. Let's do Ann Smith. She does benefit from Bootsie's death and comes to Frankenmuth frequently. She doesn't seem to have extra money. I think the killer is going to have extra money; they are smuggling. Somehow both victims threatened the smuggling ring. Mary Ellen, I'm sure the killer is very concerned about the smuggling ring being discovered."

Mary Ellen grabbed Jack's bag. "Jack is strong, has a way to move goods from one place to another. The inside of his house indicates money, and the outside is a fortress. He has a temper."

"And an alibi for Terri's death." Poppy reached over and moved his bag to the side. "Let's not discard him. I'm pretty sure he's connected."

"So finally, Jean. She seems unlikely but has the storage units all over the place. She has a personality that makes her stand out, but that could be fake. She knew Bootsie well. That's the other thing. To kill Bootsie, it had to be someone who could get close to her without alarming her."

Mary Ellen moved Jack's bag to the unlikely pile. Poppy looked at her. "I don't think Jack knew Bootsie. I think Bootsie put the wrong address into her GPS and realized it was wrong after she couldn't get in at Jack and Terri's. That coupled with the alibi makes Jack not a murderer."

Mary Ellen gathered up the bags. "We're going to meet at your house tonight to share information. I say we email Samantha. I have her in my phone from the tournament. We can tell her to drop by for a drink. It's too late to get Jean to come from Grand Rapids tonight, but we can invite her for tomorrow. We'll see who shows up."

Poppy was enthused. "I love that plan. Should we invite Ed and CJ? They are shadowing Jack Mills, but one of them might be able to come."

"That's a good idea. You text Ed. That way if he wants to alert Brent and Amanda, he can. Be vague, though. This could be a bust, and I mean that both ways."

51: ROAD TRIP

Poppy turned in Mary Ellen's driveway and Mary Ellen started to get out of the car. "Wait, it's only two o'clock. Do you want to drive around and see if we can figure out where Samantha is living? It's a shot in the dark, but maybe we'll get lucky."

"Sure, but we can't take your car; everyone in town knows your car. And my car seems a little conspicuous."

"Let's take Todd's car. He won't mind."

The girls went into the house to see Todd.

"Todd? Poppy and I would like to borrow your car. We're going to get together at Poppy's house tonight and share information. We found Jean's favorite Bay City stores and where that storage unit is. I sent the address to Ed. We'll be back by five. Todd?"

"Hang on a sec, Mary Ellen. Where are you two going?" Todd walked into the kitchen with a book in his hand. "I thought I heard you say you sent information to Ed. Aren't you done?"

Poppy smiled. Mary Ellen didn't like to tell Todd everything they were doing. She was anxious to hear how

Mary Ellen would spin this. It wouldn't be a lie; it just wouldn't be the whole truth.

"My car is low on gas. I'll fill it up tomorrow. But right now, we must run an errand out toward the outlets. I've got the fob. See you later. Could you put together a little bar basket and some snacks to take with us for the meeting at Poppy's tonight? Thanks. Love you."

Poppy buckled up and looked over at Mary Ellen. "What are you staring at?"

"I don't drive this car very often. I'm just trying to figure out what all the buttons mean."

Poppy looked a little apprehensive. "You'll be ok, right?"

Mary Ellen put the car in reverse, backed out of the driveway, and headed south.

"So, we know Buddy saw her going south toward Birch Run. My guess is she must have access to some sort of storage: a large garage, or a barn of some sort. Look for her van," Mary Ellen directed Poppy.

The girls had traveled up and down Townline and Rathbun. While they saw plenty of barns and pole barns, nothing stood out as unusual. Then they turned down Canada Road. Poppy yelled to Mary Ellen, "Stop! There's Luanne, Betsy, and MJ. They walk every day and all live around here. Let's ask them if they know anything."

Poppy rolled her window down. "Hi, girls, are you out for your walk?"

Luanne waved at Mary Ellen. "We didn't recognize your car. How are you both?"

"We're good. Listen, we're looking for a friend's house. We lost the directions and she's not answering the phone. Samantha? She just moved here from Grand Rapids. I think she might have a barn on her property. Does that sound familiar?"

Betsy grimaced. "She might be my new neighbor. Is she really your friend? She put up all kinds of DO NOT TRESPASS signs and has made it very clear she is not neighborly. I brought her over some cookies. She said she doesn't eat sweets, 'thanks anyway,' and closed the door."

MJ pointed down the road. "It's the third house down. Good luck."

"Thanks, girls. See you soon."

Mary Ellen slowly drove down the street. "It's that house, with the pole barn. Should we look inside? There is no van in the driveway. Just a quick look?"

The girls left Todd's car on the side of the road and walked quickly to the barn. "There is a window on the door. Look in; I'll keep a look out. Hurry up, Poppy."

"There are boxes and crates with straw in them. I can't really see much else. Let's get out of here. We'll share all this tonight."

No one noticed the small camera that was on the corner of the roof.

Poppy called Ed right away to tell him he might find what they needed at this location, and she and Mary Ellen headed back to Poppy's house as planned.

Ed said, "We're on it right now, Poppy. Thanks. We've looked in every other storage unit that might have a tie to any of this and came up empty. You girls keep your fingers crossed! Where's Barney, by the way?"

"I think he's at my house right now," Poppy said.

"Ok. I'm sure we'll all wind up in the same place at some point." Ed hung up.

52: Comparing Notes

Barney pulled into Poppy's driveway, noticing Mary Ellen's car first thing. Hopefully, they could fill each other in on any news they had acquired that day. Barney opened the garage door and parked next to the Range Rover.

Everyone but Todd was seated in the living room. Barney greeted them and noticed a few dining room chairs had been pulled in to form a circle. "Are we expecting more people?"

Just then, Todd walked into the room with a plate of beautifully decorated cookies from local legendary baker, Dawn Barrett. "Hi, Barney. Want a drink, coffee, tea, something stronger? Dawn delivered these earlier. She said they were from a canceled order, and thought we might enjoy them. I think they might have been for a bachelor party. Some are a little risqué, but so delicious."

Todd put the cookies on the table. Everyone leaned over to check them out. Mary Ellen started giggling. "My goodness, they are interesting. Dawn has managed to get the point across without being vulgar. I'll take the girl with the fan. So, Barney, are Ed and CJ coming?"

Barney snagged a girl in a martini glass. "I texted Ed. I know they are taking turns keeping an eye on Jack and checking out some storage places. Hopefully, he is going to lead us to the smuggler and the killer. I have a feeling they are one and the same, but I'm keeping an open mind. What did you and Poppy find out today?"

Mary Ellen had a mouthful of cookie, so she motioned to Poppy to talk. "We drove to Millington to track Jean Roy's favorite antique stores. On our way, we spotted Samantha in her truck. We found her unloading boxes behind Meijer. She was not happy to see us. But it did appear that she was indeed making deliveries. We then went to Millington and discovered that Jean does have things delivered to a storage unit, the ones right off 46, on Gera Road. We were hoping that Ed could get into the unit with a warrant. Mary Ellen, would you agree that both Jean and Samantha are still suspects?"

"Yes, we still need something solid to eliminate either of them. I'm still not so sure Dennis Van der Veer is innocent of Bootsie's death. I do not see the connection between Bootsie and Terri Mills. I know Bootsie was at the Mills's house, but that can be explained by an incorrect entry into the GPS."

The doorbell chimed and the friends all looked at each other. Barney was closest to the door. As he got up, he said, "Maybe that's Ed or CJ."

Instead, to everyone's surprise, in came Jean Roy. "Hello, are you having a party? I stopped at Mary Ellen's house, but no one was there. As I was driving out of the neighborhood, I saw her car here, so I took a chance. Mary Ellen, I just wanted to bring you this little gift as a token of my appreciation for the tournament. We had such a great time. Do I know everyone? I'm Jean Roy, the maven of Grand Rapids, only due to the death of my dear friend, Bootsie Van der Veer."

"Jean, what a surprise. You remember Poppy and Barney from the tournament. And this is my husband, Todd."

Todd nodded. "Would you like a coffee?"

Jean said, "Yes, please." She sat down in the nearest chair and looked at the table.

"Is this a swinger party? Have I interrupted a swinger party?" Jean was pointing at the cookie plate. "I had no idea."

Mary Ellen stood up quickly. "No, these are cookies from a canceled bachelor party that our baker friend thought we could eat."

Todd came back into the room with Jean's coffee. "By the way, I just let Babycakes out. She clearly wanted to go."

Poppy jumped up. "Let her out? Let her out where?"

"I opened the sliding door, and she ran out. She seemed quite excited."

Barney said, "I'll go get her. You all stay here and chat."

Mary Ellen looked at her husband. "Did you do that on purpose? Babycakes has a special dog door into a fenced area. Todd?"

Todd shook his head. "No, I just thought she went out the big door. Poppy, I am so sorry. For no reason that I understood, she just seemed to want to put some distance between her and me."

He stood up and gave Poppy a hug. Jean looked horrified. Poppy rolled her eyes and accidentally stepped on Todd's vulnerable big toe sticking out of his sandal.

Poppy said, "It's happened before, although just opening a door and letting a dog out isn't the best dog management; no offense, Todd. She normally barks and runs around the city park that backs up to the houses in this neighborhood, gets hungry or curious, and comes in. Barney's her favorite person right now, so he'll probably wrangle her back in this direction."

Indeed, barking was happening. In fact, it was a cacophony of disparate noises. Babycakes's barking around in circles was amplified by at least three other dogs defending their turf by barking back, but they weren't free to race around like Babycakes. Barney's voice would occasionally rise above the racket as he literally ran after the dog, a technique absolutely designed to avoid catching her.

Meantime, Poppy's watch dinged with an incoming message signal. She took a quick look and noticed that Amazon had reported that Dennis had never ordered or searched for concentrated caffeine. And neither had Jean, Jack, or Samantha, who didn't even have an Amazon account. This felt like saying Samantha still told time with a pocket watch, thought Poppy. That wasn't definitive proof they never obtained any, but it was evidence no one on the suspect list got it from Amazon. Not, at least, in their own names.

Barney was outside making little smacking noises as though he were eating something good to entice Babycakes to rejoin them. Poppy was amazed he hadn't just taken a cookie with him, but no doubt he was afraid to leave Babycakes on her own.

What they didn't know was that right then, CJ and Ed were making their way back to town, having been on what felt like a wild goose chase for a good part of the day, but that had finally paid off in the end after their talk with Poppy and Mary Ellen. They weren't coming back for the cookies. They were coming back, they hoped, to make arrests if their suspects were still around.

Things were weird and noisy, and Poppy and Mary Ellen still didn't have confirmation of who the killer or killers were at this point.

Poppy felt especially bad about all the noise and chaos going on in the park because her next-door neighbors, Tim and Sue, quiet people and good friends, were trying to enjoy their own hot tub now. She noticed they opted for cranking up some music to drown out Babycakes and all the other dogs living around the park. There were too many things drawing her attention. Getting her dog into the house was a pretty high priority. And she wasn't exactly sure why Jean was here or how to get rid of her. She glanced at Jean chewing on another cookie.

The girls knew they were getting close with the information they gave Ed and CJ, and wanted to see where it led them. They both knew it would be great for their private investigation business to help wrap this up.

53: Someone Comes Up Missing

Jean, who was bizarrely fascinated with Dawn's cookies, asked if she could have one for the road. Poppy was so glad at the mention of "road" that she chose the biggest cookie on the plate and wrapped it up carefully for Jean to take with her.

"Great," said Mary Ellen, herself anxious to say adios to the party crasher, if that was what she was.

Just then, there came a gentle knock on the door from the back deck. And it occurred to everyone that the park had gone quiet. Yet Babycakes and Barney weren't back yet. Poppy went to the back door and found Tim next door, dripping wet, holding a smiling Babycakes in his arms. And she seemed fine with that. Tim and Sue had always treated her right. In fact, Poppy had decided her dog had more friends than she did.

Tim and Babycakes stepped inside, and Tim explained that he and Sue had fired up the grill for hamburgers and they always made a couple extra. Tim decided to unwind in the hot tub, and this was why he was dripping wet in a swimsuit.

"Sorry to bother everyone," he said, as Poppy, Mary Ellen, and Todd all stared spellbound at Babycakes looking perfectly happy being held. She was wet too. "I was surprised to see Babycakes running around our back yard since that's never happened before. She came over, I think, because there was an extra burger on the grill. Did you know she can jump really high? She flew through the air, snagged a leftover burger—oh, don't worry about it; we didn't mind—and when I called her, she came right over and leaped into the hot tub with me! I had no idea a dog shaped like her with those short little legs could swim, but she was paddling away there. I thought I should bring her home. She's a nice visitor, but I know she's supposed to stay in her own yard, and we don't want her to get lost."

Poppy was stunned that her dog stole a hamburger, went for a swim, snuggled up with the next-door neighbor, and smiled about it with absolutely no shame. In fact, she looked like she was certain that treats and lots of "good girls" were in order for some reason. But then again, Todd did let her out the door like that was a normal event.

"Oh, good grief! Thank you so much, Tim. We've had Barney out looking for her—she ordinarily races over to see him but apparently, she didn't this time. Must have been the burger. I'm so happy we aren't still on a dog hunt! Can I offer you a cookie? And one for Sue, too, of course?" Actually, Poppy was shocked it was Tim standing there with Babycakes and not Sue, since Tim had often seemed a little nervous around the dog.

"Oh, wow," said Tim. "Did Dawn bake those?"

"She sure did. She had a party order that got canceled, I was looking for some good cookies but didn't preorder, and we ended up with these incredibly cool cookies."

"Nice! Yeah, I'll take two of those. Sue and I both love them."

Again, Poppy packed up cookies and passed them along to Tim. While she had been anxious to get rid of Jean, she was always happy to see the next-door neighbors.

Tim took off with the cookies, and Poppy dried off her dog.

Todd said, "Well, where is Barney? Why isn't he with Babycakes? Why isn't he back here at the house? What's going on here exactly?" And that was the moment it struck Poppy that Barney was gone.

Not gone in that usual way of his of blowing in and out of town or the country or the continent, but just gone, and she was worried. After all the noise and racing around in the park, it was strangely quiet and dark. Right then, Ed and CJ entered the house without even knocking.

"Good news and bad news, everyone. The good news is that Mary Ellen and Poppy's tip about where to locate goods that were smuggled in was spot on. We found all kinds of tiny to fairly large carved ivory statuettes in that pole barn. And that was linked directly to Samantha.

"The bad news is there was a live camera on the corner of that building and Samantha could see us enter and call in the feds—after all, this is their case—at least the smuggling part—and Samantha absolutely lost it. She was clocked heading back into Frankenmuth after collecting Jack Mills at close to 100 mph, and not the opposite direction as we might have thought.

"One more thing: while searching the pole barn, not only did we find smuggled goods, but we found what will surely turn out to be the small container of pure caffeine and syringes that were used to kill Bootsie."

Poppy gasped. She definitely had taken Bootsie's death personally. "Why is she here in town and not far in the opposite direction?"

Just at that moment, they heard Barney's voice from the far end of the park, saying, "Babycakes! Babycakes! Come get a treat! Come to your Uncle Barney!"

No one had thought about Barney still searching for the supposedly lost dog. Instead, they assumed he'd pop back into the house any second.

But his voice was a target, and the next sound was two gunshots.

54: The Aftermath

Poppy remembered the sinking feeling she had about Barney helping the feds on this case—but she had no idea how much undercover work he had been doing for the past five years. Later, Poppy thought, that was why they called it undercover. Although she thought she understood what it involved, she never knew the extent of his work. And she never knew what she didn't know. Ideal undercover work meant keeping the circle tight.

Before Poppy could put together one more thought, a lot of feds were in the park, guided by the gunshots. No one could quickly amass what looked like an army of cops like the feds. Everyone in the house also wanted to run to the scene, but they were stopped since it was still an active shooting scene.

"We've got this," hollered Brent Weiss. "Please stand down until this is all secured."

In short, several critical things happened. First, Barney had in fact been shot twice. Samantha was furious that her relentless flirting had no effect on Barney and fired on him as soon as she heard him. She knew her game was up, and she wasn't pleased. She very much wanted to kill Barney before her inevitable arrest—what was one more murder conviction? What saved Barney from sudden death was that Samantha's trigger finger was guided by sound rather than light, certainly imprecise, relatively speaking. Although any gunshot wound was bad, expert assistance was close. One of the very few trauma-one emergency centers in the state of Michigan, and the only one in the region, was right down the road, in Flint.

Poppy wasn't about to stand down—after all, she quickly reasoned—she worked for Barney, not the feds. She immediately ran for the Range Rover, and much to her surprise, CJ jumped in beside her. Just as she was about to slam the door, Chuckie flew into the car determined not to be left out of whatever was happening.

Poppy kept the Range Rover lights off and snaked the car around the block trying to get closer to Barney as the feds closed in on Samantha and Jack. Poppy knew where Barney was almost surely located and how to get there since it was more or less her backyard. Jack could see that the main target was Samantha. In the dark, he bolted toward the house, assuming everyone had left.

As they came around the second corner, Poppy and CJ could see Samantha, still in a murderous rage, crawling behind trees toward Barney. She was so focused on her quarry that the first time she noticed CJ was when she felt the Glock 22 service weapon touch the side of her head.

At that point, the feds caught up and cuffed Samantha, arresting her for murder for starters.

Barney was surrounded by women—CJ, Poppy, and Amanda Weiss. The best thing they heard was Barney saying,

"Did you stop her? Is she in custody?" And he was assured by Amanda that she wasn't a threat to anyone anymore.

Poppy held his hand for reassurance for both of them while CJ called in a "man down / gunshot wound" report. CJ told Barney that a Medivac chopper was on its way from Hurley Hospital in Flint and would land at the parking lot of Covenant Med Express not two blocks from where they were.

While all this emergency care was aimed at Barney, the federal team, while clearly having Samantha under control, were nonetheless impressed with her tirade.

Samantha threw the worst apoplectic fit, at least since Al Capone died of it, in the history of federal arrests. Since everything was recorded, all of it was caught on record. "Get your hands off me, you filthy bastards," she yelled. "Did I kill him? Is Barney dead, I hope? He's the worst 'date,' if you can call it that, I've ever had. My gun misfired! I despise technology. I hate you all! I'm so fed up with all of you!" screamed Samantha, who might have been the worst-behaved person detained by these particular feds that they had ever seen. "I despise bumbling Bootsie and tattletale Terri. What irritating women." With considerable efforts, she was hauled off under heavy guard to Saginaw County's jail, where she was kept in isolation.

Jack, in the meantime, didn't have the clear getaway path he was hoping for. Instead, Ed, Mary Ellen, and Todd saw his approach and Ed yelled, "Stop, drop any weapons, and get on your knees." As he did that, Mary Ellen, surprising everyone, came up with a whip and concluded the take down.

Todd said to his wife, "Where in the world did that whip come from, Mary Ellen?"

She responded, "Poppy uses it to discourage squirrels who annoy Babycakes."

Todd and Ed both said, "Oh."

The charges at both arraignments sobered Samantha and Jack right up: two counts of first-degree murder, one count of attempted murder, resisting arrest, and a laundry list of other crimes they could charge them with.

There they stayed until the agents Weiss could securely move both detainees to the federal detention center south of Ann Arbor, one of only two in the state.

It was Samantha's good luck that the federal team wasn't going by sound instead of sight, despite the moonless night. The agents Weiss had regular unlit rifles in case this fire power were needed, and could depend on the rest of the team's pistol-mounted lights for good target identification. Their pistols with lights attached under the barrels lit up the park sufficiently to identify the right target, a good thing since CJ and Poppy had ignored the "stand down" instruction, but no one was talking about that. Adrenalin ran high.

Both Ed and CJ were independently thinking the city might want to come up with more competitive firepower, since obviously it was hard to say what even a small town of five thousand residents might face. This town was very good at fundraisers.

CJ, in her capacity as a police detective, rode the chopper to Flint with Barney and stuck with him until he was released the next day. His wounds, as it turns out, weren't life-threatening. Someone at the emergency room even came up with a small crate for Chuckie who stuck by CJ all the way, snarling and snapping at anyone too close.

And at last, Frankenmuth did what it was extremely good at: it made sure its citizens understood what happened, that everyone was ok, and that all questions were responded to (no matter how redundant).

And for part of that, Ed's upcoming press release would do the job. He had become good at these, what to say and not say, and how to assure public confidence. The news at 6:00 p.m. the next day would have a good audience.

55: NEWS AT 6:00

Mayor Ackerman, not in her trademark dirndl but rather a conservative business suit, took the lead in front of the cameras from all over the state and beyond for the 6:00 news. "Following two homicides in Frankenmuth that were originally thought to be unrelated, arrests have been made in this complex case. Chief Ed Swartz is here to make a statement and take your questions. Thank you for coming."

She exited the stage to view the press conference from an office in the police station. Ed knew to keep his information down to a few basics because the reporters would pepper him with questions no matter how much detail he gave ahead of time. So, he opened the floor for questions after a quick explanation of how the two murders were related and that two people were now in jail.

Poppy was tuned in from home. Barney was out and Poppy assumed he was taking advantage of CJ's surprisingly effective nursing talents. He certainly needed to take it easy for a while.

Poppy had let her mind wander and apparently missed a couple things, but her attention was drawn to a reporter from Flint asking, "So, is it true or untrue that a private detective in town—Poppy someone? —drove over a Mah Jongg player from Grand Rapids? What's that got to do with coffee, exactly?"

Ed internally sighed but he had developed some patience for redundancy through press experience. As he was giving the accurate story of how Bootsie died, at Poppy's house Babycakes landed on the floor with a thud as Poppy sprang out of her seat yelling at the TV. When would people quit asking if she ran over Bootsie! Babycakes wandered off to get a drink of water, already bored with the question.

Mary Ellen and Todd were just about to sit down to some homemade soup—a favorite of both of them—but they turned on the news. "Boy, Poppy isn't going to appreciate that one question," Todd commented.

"Too right," said Mary Ellen. "We need to get away. Let's finally take that cross–country trip we've been talking about. Can you work your phone magic and get us out of town within a day or two?"

"My Sweets, consider it done." Todd enjoyed working on pleasant tasks like taking an out–of–town trip. He prided himself on securing fast arrangements at good prices no matter how much time he had to spend on hold.

"I don't think they've mentioned the feds," Todd said. Mary Ellen just shrugged. She was convinced now that feds were rarely mentioned.

Ed was starting to get tired of questions like, "Is it still safe to visit Frankenmuth?" In a Poppy-esque line of logic, Ed pointed out that if you looked at the law of averages throughout the decades, it's one of the safest places on the globe.

Indeed, Poppy was right that CJ was making sure Barney was getting pain pills on time and nutritional food at her place. Even Chuckie was settled into bed with the two of them. If he felt safe with CJ, he felt both safe and spoiled with CJ and Barney—plus Barney clearly needed his guard dog services, and Chuckie was glad to oblige. What Chuckie didn't know was that CJ and Barney were planning their own vacation to Africa. Barney couldn't wait to show her around.

At her house, Poppy locked up. Babycakes was already snoring, and Poppy headed for bed, too.

Ed was satisfied that the reporters got the basic information they came for but not much more.

Citizens in both Frankenmuth and Grand Rapids were ready for a good night's sleep.

●●●

The next day, the agents Weiss were out of town before anyone saw them go, except one person. They stopped at the Kaffee Haus for one more great cup of coffee before departing and noticed Father Bob having a solitary moment, sipping his own cappuccino by the back door dressed in "regular" clothes. They looked at each other and knew it was maybe the only chance they'd ever get. Amanda spoke to the priest. "Thanks for all the help on that last case a couple years ago." They kept walking, knowing no response would be coming.

In not too long at all, Fr. Bob would be enjoying an espresso at an outdoor café just steps away from the Pantheon in Rome. It even had heaters near the tables in case of cool weather. Of course, he listened to Ed's press conference, the first comprehensive summary he had heard of the latest murders in Frankenmuth, and he knew for a fact that mention of the federal authorities had been left out of Ed's summary.

As the feds exited the Kaffee Haus for the last time in the foreseeable future, the priest looked down at his copy of LeCarré's final novel and smiled just a little to himself. It was fascinating, he reflected, how the most unexpected opportunities presented themselves in retirement. He was known as "our man in Rome" in more than one circle. He checked his watch. He had his own plane to catch.

Epilogue

Mary Ellen parked next to the Covered Bridge Shop. She looked around the parking lot for Poppy's Range Rover and grabbed her purse and a gift bag from her car. The shop had a great bar area. Poppy had suggested a drink and a catch-up chat. Mary Ellen and Todd had taken a three-week, cross-country road trip, and although they had texted, this was the first opportunity to rehash the events of that spring.

Mary Ellen pushed open the door and was surprised to see Poppy already seated at a table. "Hello, traveler. How are you? I ordered you a glass of Sauvignon Blanc. They have a few specialty drinks if you want to try one?"

"Poppy, it's great to see you. The wine is perfect, thank you. Where is your car? Is it in the shop again!"

Poppy shrugged. "It needed a tune-up. You know they have concierge service. They'll deliver it right back here when it's ready. I love my Range Rover. How were your adventures?"

"It's a great car when you actually have it. Anyway, the trip was wonderful. We were able to visit four national parks. They are truly treasures. We saw family and friends and have decided to stay put for the entire summer. The thought of sleeping in one more hotel has no appeal at all. I did bring you this." Mary Ellen handed her the gift bag.

Poppy pulled out a rectangular package. She read the contents out loud, laughing. "It's an inflatable bumper for most makes of car. Too soon, ME, too soon. Things here have been quiet."

"Samantha and Jack will both go on trial in the next month, Samantha for two murders and international smuggling, Jack for smuggling. Sadly, the smuggling ring was designed so each person only knew one or two other people in the chain. Samantha will spend the rest of her life in prison. Jack seems to be a little cog in the big wheel."

"Jack was an accomplice and knew the ivory was illegal. Thankfully, his daughter, Marcia, is being taken care of by her aunt. I spoke with Maddie, Marcia's teacher at List. Marcia loves her school and has a new puppy, a little French bulldog mix named Frankie. They got it from the Midwest Boston Terrier Rescue group. Imagine losing your mother and having a father in prison." Mary Ellen shook her head.

"On a better note, Ed said they found my Mah Jongg set. Samantha had quite a collection of sets. I'll get mine back before we travel to Grand Rapids for our return tournament."

Poppy looked surprised. "They still want a tournament? I bought a travel Mah Jongg set to take on my river cruise. I plan on winning that tournament."

"Jean texted me while we were gone to suggest one. She's working for Van der Veer Electric as an interior lighting designer. Anne, Bootsie's sister, co-owns the business with

Dennis. They are doing quite well and expanding to more areas in Michigan."

Poppy took a sip of her drink. "Barney has recovered from his gunshot wounds. I know he has been in contact with the WWF in Switzerland. Killing elephants for ivory will not stop until the demand for ivory is diminished. He feels very strongly about getting rid of ivory trading. In fact, he and CJ have gone to Africa. It holds a very special place in his heart. CJ left Chuckie with the Lists. Munchie is delighted to have a partner in crime."

"Is he still planning on moving here? Do you think he'll move in with CJ?"

"He bought a place over on Tuscola Road. It's being renovated while they are gone. They'll still be able to do their morning 'walks.'" Poppy made air quotes.

"Speaking of walks, I want to go to Charlin's Book Nook, the used bookstore. I would like an older book by Louise Penny, and I suspect they'll have it. Join me?"

Poppy stood up, checked her phone, and chuckled. "Sure, then I have to go home. My car will be delivered in an hour."

As Poppy and Mary Ellen walked out, they saw a brochure advertising Oktoberfest. Mary Ellen took one and put it in her purse. "I love Oktoberfest. Todd has invited an eclectic group of friends for the weekend from high school, college, and work. Hopefully, they all enjoy singing, dancing, and beer, and create no drama."

Poppy hesitated a moment. "I used to think there was never drama in Frankenmuth. Now I'm wondering if we are attracting it."

They exchanged uneasy looks.

Poppy and Mary Ellen's List of Mah Jongg Resources
For Those Who Want to Learn More about this Great Game

1. What is the "annual card" and do I need one? You need a "card" to play American style Mah Jongg. This is a game with many different versions around the globe. The National Mah Jongg League in New York City creates a new card every year that changes what winning hands consist of. If you don't have a card, you don't play—and you want to play! (nationalmahjonggleague.org)

2. What is a rack? Racks are part of the game equipment. Every set comes with four racks, one for each player. Players place their tiles on the slanted part of the rack so no one can see them. When they expose tiles, they are placed on the flat part of the rack.

3. What are these tiles? American play needs 152 tiles to play a game. Each tile is marked like a deck of cards showing what sort of tile it is. Instead of kings, queens, and jacks, Mah Jongg tiles have symbols like flowers, winds, and dragons.

4. Dead Hand: If it becomes impossible for a player to make one of the hands on the card and other players can see that, anyone can call that player's hand "dead." They can no longer play until the next game. Players cannot call themselves dead. (Just keep playing and pretend you're not dead.)

5. Jokers: Each set has eight Jokers that can substitute for a tile you need. However, no matter what, Jokers cannot be used as a single or part of a pair. Period. Full Stop. Don't do it.

6. Walls: All four players help create walls at the start of each hand. This is in place of shuffling and other means of distributing tiles at the start.

7. "We play a friendly game." Pro-tip. That statement is the start of passionate arguments. Some people ignore some of the rules because they play a "friendly game." Others see that adhering to the rules IS a friendly game because everyone plays by the same rules.

8. Mah Jongg That's It: This is the biggest, most informative, and most fun Facebook page about the game of American style Mah Jongg. This site is always growing and has tens of thousands of participants. If you have a FB account, this is great to follow. You'll learn a lot about the game, get questions answered (very fast) and feel part of an amazing group of players.

9. Elaine Sanders' *The Beginner's Guide to Mah Jongg*. If you are a new player (or even if you aren't), this is a wonderful book to own. Do not buy it as a Kindle download even though you can. You need to be able to see colors to learn this game properly.

10. *In Search of Bubbe Fischer* by Karen Gooen. When you are beyond figuring out basic play and ready to advance a bit, this book is fabulous. It is a combination of memoir and game strategy and is so well written, it's hard to put down. Then there's the pithy advice that really will help with game strategy, like Bubbe's unforgettable advice, "If you can't win, don't lose." Believe it or not, that's often a choice, and an important strategy, in Mah Jongg.

To know this game is to love it! Both Poppy and Mary Ellen recommend it.

Acknowledgements

From Susan: Thank you to gretchen, Jason, and Sheehan for your interest, suggestions, and support. And to my wonderful husband and unpaid intern, Mel—you are the best.

From Roz: To James, Gladys, Ski, Zane, and Migi, endless gratitude for being so close even when you're so far away and making that trip home. And to Crissy who is inspiring in so many ways.

Thanks to our friends at Mission Point Press who get us through the process.

Thanks to an amazing community of friends who are loaded with ideas, including those who found the time to read for us: Joan Ramm, Karen List, Denise Hill, and Ethel Richards.

And much appreciation to the wonderful Frankenmuth businesses who carry our books, the Covered Bridge Shop, Charlin's Book Nook, The Frankenmuth Kaffee Haus, and the Frankenmuth Historical Museum.

ABOUT THE AUTHORS AND ILLUSTRATOR

Roz Weedman

Roz Weedman lives in the tourist town of Frankenmuth, Michigan. She worked for thirteen years as a legal secretary, continued her education at the University of Michigan, and eventually retired from her position as a professor of English after twenty years. Her teaching career focused on writing and American literature. For pleasure, she reads mysteries from Louise Penny, Anthony Horowitz, Ian Rankin, Agatha Christie, and other masters of the genre. Roz loves nothing more than playing Mah Jongg with her friends and grandkids. She believes road trips are the best trips. If you're in Frankenmuth, she's easy to find. Her white minivan with the Mahj license plate will be parked askew somewhere in town.

Cookie Weedman

Cookie Weedman, rescued during the pandemic by Midwest Boston Terrier Rescue, and the inspiration for Babycakes.

Susan Todd

Susan Todd lives in Frankenmuth, Michigan, with Mel, her husband of over fifty years. After being a stay-at-home mom, she went back to get her teaching degree. She started her work at the same college her son was attending. After graduating, Susan and Mel moved to Frankenmuth, where she taught elementary and middle school for eleven years. Since retiring, they enjoy traveling both abroad and in the US. They have a daughter, gretchen, and a son, Jason. If you travel to Frankenmuth and see a silver-blue convertible zipping around town, give Susan a wave.

Lane Trabalka, illustrator

Lane Trabalka is a visual arts 2D concentration student in twelfth grade at an arts and sciences school in Saginaw. She enjoys noticing, mulling over, and sometimes drawing the finer details of the world around her.

Made in the USA
Monee, IL
09 December 2024

72930195R00152